MOSCOW BY NIGHTMARE

MOSCOW BY NIGHTMARE

Joyce L. Shub

Coward, McCann & Geoghegan
New York

First American Edition 1973

SBN: 698-10527-3

Library of Congress Catalog Card Number: 72-29416

PRINTED IN THE UNITED STATES OF AMERICA

To Russia with Love

Chapter One

Yuri should not have come. He was in Moscow illegally. The cocktail party was suspect. He had never met the host. Nor did he expect to know any of the guests—except perhaps for Vannie Tomkins.

Yuri had intended merely to walk Lydia to the house and let her go up alone. She could have managed the business herself. Then, impulsively, he followed her in.

Had he reflected a moment as they rode up in the mirrored elevator or paused in the cluttered penthouse passageway, he might have turned back. Instead, he reached over Lydia's head and pushed open Rabichov's massive Byzantine door.

It was too late. Through the noise and smoke, curious eyes inspected the tall stranger. Three of the guests recognized Yuri as the general's nephew. And one among them already knew that his uncle, General Pyotr Alexandrovich Zhalkov, commander of the Leningrad Military District, was dead.

While Lydia slipped unobtrusively into the crowd, Yuri hesitated at the doorway, searching for the lively face of Vannie Tomkins. Yuri glimpsed the back of her head, her violent red hair, as she moved toward the window. Vannie had spotted him first and had turned away, puzzled. *Why had Lydia brought him?*

Vannie knew him two months, but only as "Yuri from Leningrad." She had found him at a corner table in her friend Lydia's basement room, a wiry, sandy-haired stranger firing a large piece of malachite with an acetylene torch. The rock had burst into a steamy liquid, jumping under the unrelenting heat like a bead of mercury, its secret imperfections transformed into fiery, swirling colors. Abruptly, Yuri had handed her the blowtorch, his cool blue eyes searching her face. "Why don't you try it?" he asked. "No, thanks"—Vannie smiled— "it's safer watching."

A few days later, when Vannie had dropped by again, Lydia had been staring intently, mallet in hand, at a half-finished clay bust. Yuri had silently motioned Vannie over to the corner table, covered by his collection of semiprecious stones. Quietly, he had pointed out the sinuous striations of each specimen. A week afterward, he taught her how to hold the torch and melt rock to its essence. Yet, in all their afternoons together, Vannie had never asked Yuri's last name, nor why he had left Leningrad.

Nor had she questioned the circumstances of Sasha Rabichov's unusual party. The day before, a pale Saturday afternoon, at that undecided hour between a last coffee and a first vodka, the grating ring of the telephone had brought her running into the bedroom. Sasha's voice was not the usual cryptic mumble of most Russians who feared identification on the tapped telephone lines. Rabichov spoke loud and clear. He was a bohemian of good breeding who, with a dozen English phrases and heavy-lidded eyes, could awaken the Slavic heart under the shirtwaist of any American woman who rested in awe of his golden icons.

"Vannie, darling, this is Rabichov. I've just gotten a visa for Paris. I must celebrate. Tomorrow at four o'clock. I shall show my whole art collection to my friends. Why don't you come early?"

"My husband is in Moscow now. May I bring him?"

"Certainly. I'd like to meet him. Come at three and I'll give you both the grand tour."

Vannie was delighted. This was their first invitation to a Russian party in seven months. Since the Soviet invasion of Czechoslovakia the past August, there had been a social freeze in Moscow. Foreign embassy receptions were sober, quieter. Few Soviet officials were invited; still fewer came, barely remaining long enough to pay diplomatic respects. With the winter, a weary, edgy bitterness settled over the city. Vannie hoped that Rabichov's party, like Moscow's last snow flurries, signaled the start of a friendlier spring.

Ken Tomkins, ten years older, was wary of his wife's enthusiasms. He had to fly to Rome Monday to meet his foreign editor, he said, and needed Sunday night to pack. Vannie promised to leave the party early. Ken remained skeptical. "It might be a good story for you," Vannie prodded. "Maybe the KGB will come and close down the exhibition."

9

"Maybe the KGB is sponsoring it," Ken had replied. Suspicious of Sasha's unique collection of "underground" paintings—art officially disapproved by the Soviet authorities but privately shown, and sold, to curious foreigners—Ken had long evaded invitations to the famous studio.

That evening, in the red-carpeted rotunda of the Bolshoi Theater, they had discovered Lydia, half-hidden behind a marble pillar. The diminutive sculptress seemed preoccupied. Surprised that Vannie wished to attend tomorrow's art exhibition, Lydia dismissed Rabichov as a dilettante who collected everything because he knew the value of nothing.

Yet Ken had finally relented. "If it's the kind of party I think it is," he said when they returned home from the theater, "I'd better come along to keep you out of trouble."

"What kind of trouble could I possibly get into?" Vannie asked, unbuttoning her blue jersey. "I follow all the rules. I don't ask questions. I don't repeat gossip. And I don't buy or sell on the black market."

Pleased by her virtuous declaration, she slipped into a transparent, flesh-colored nightgown. "What more could anyone want from me?" she asked, hands on her hips, smiling.

Ken puffed as he zipped off his fur-lined boots, his back to her. "Not more, Vannie. Maybe less," he said. "You keep visiting all those underground painters."

"Don't make it sound so sneaky, Ken. They're simple, nonpolitical bohemians."

"Nobody in this country is nonpolitical," he retorted, getting up to pull a gray sweater over his head.

"Me! Me! I'm unpolitical," she flared. "And my friends like me just the way I am."

He finally looked at her, standing in regal fury beside the bed. "Well, well," he said solemnly. "So do I—just the way you are."

Vannie slipped under the feather quilt. "I know" —she smiled—"but you have so little time these days."

The telephone rang. Startled, Vannie swiftly reached across the bed to answer. Once again, it was the familiar operator's voice: "Gospodin Tomkins, New York calling."

Vannie handed Ken the phone with its long cord. "The home office, darling," she said, pointing to the living room. "Do remind them that four o'clock their time is midnight in Moscow. Normal people are in bed." She switched off the light before he had closed the door.

The Tomkinses set out for Rabichov's directly after lunch the next day. It was almost April, and gray snow still covered the courtyard of the foreigners' compound in which they lived. Their apartment was at the last entrance of one of two long, yellow-brick, ten-story buildings that faced each other, at right angles to the avenue. A narrow black-tar roadway encircled the courtyard between the two buildings. A high mesh fence enclosed both apartment houses, forcing all residents to enter and leave the compound in full view of the glass observation window of the Soviet sentry box stationed near the avenue entrance.

11

In mild weather, two blue-coated Soviet militiamen, with pistols bulging in black holsters, would plant themselves in their high black boots outside the wooden sentry box. Today the wind was raw, promising snow by nightfall, and the Tomkinses could only discern two pairs of eyes and two red-trimmed, black-peaked caps observing them as they left the compound and hailed a taxi.

Rabichov's studio resembled neither the claustrophobic foreigners' compound nor the impoverished rooms of other Russians Vannie had visited. It spread out along the penthouse floor of a well-kept flagstone prewar building that towered over two adjacent foreign embassies. The Tomkinses took the mirrored elevator up twelve floors, climbed a narrow flight of stairs, and then picked their way among planks of lumber cluttering the hall. "Sasha is always remodeling," Vannie explained.

Just before the studio, there was a closet-sized kitchen, in which masses of hors d'oeuvres were piled on an assortment of trays and plates. There were red and black caviar arranged in checkerboard patterns; creamy sturgeon on dark pumpernickel, topped with thin slivers of onion; mounds of moist radishes in deep crystal bowls.

The door to the studio itself had been carted away from a monastery in Novgorod. Sasha had had the wall frame raised and rounded to meet the door's Byzantine contour. He had left the large, hand-forged studs a dull charcoal to impress visitors with its antiquity.

The door was ajar when the Tomkinses arrived. Sasha, in a wine-colored blazer with a paisley ascot tucked into an open white shirt, stood with his back to an enormous studio window, a long Russian cigarette poised between his fingers. His arms were open in a wide gesture of explanation toward an Empire chair of dark-green brocade with massive oak armrests.

"Ah, there you are," he suddenly cried, crossing the polished studio parquet, his arms still spread for an all-embracing kiss on both cheeks.

Helping Vannie off with her coat, he playfully tugged a lock of her hair. "Fantastic—I must find a painter to do justice to that color." It was what he always said, but Vannie was embarrassed hearing it in front of Ken.

As the two men shook hands, Vannie slipped on her party shoes and threw her sheepskin boots into a plastic shopping bag. "Here, let me take it," Sasha offered. "I'll hide it in the kitchen behind the refrigerator."

He left Ken to admire the whitewashed, panel-trimmed studio with its vaulted thirty-foot ceiling. Returning, he led them toward the green brocade chair.

"You've heard me speak of Simone Durand, haven't you, Vannie?"

Her short black curls barely reached the oak-bordered headrest, but the size of the chair could not diminish the firm presence of this square-shouldered woman encased in a brown tweed suit. Perhaps, with her clear skin and firmly curved lips, she had once been handsome. But middle age had puffed the lids above the cool gray eyes and pulled taut the lines along her mouth.

"Yes, of course. You used to live in Moscow. I'm so happy to meet you at last. This is my husband, Ken Tomkins."

"You are Kenneth L. Tomkins, the American journalist?" asked Simone Durand.

Ken nodded absently as he stared up at Sasha's icon collection. Enraptured faces displaced from abandoned churches were massed on the walls opposite the studio window, the sunlight picking up antique glints of red and gold.

"Madame Durand, weren't you the first collector of underground art in Moscow?" Vannie asked.

Simone Durand smiled. She had pearly teeth. "How nice to have left a reputation here! But these painters were mere children when I discovered them. That was fifteen years ago."

"Sasha told me you have a priceless collection of their early paintings in Paris." Vannie leaned forward, eager to catch every nuance.

Simone tilted her head coyly. "Oh, I don't know. It is really Sasha who has collected their mature work. Shall we go upstairs and see what he has put together?"

Simone led the way up the winding staircase. "Some Frenchwoman," Ken whispered to Vannie, "her accent is straight from Minsk."

The open gallery, jutting out below the vaulted ceiling, stretched the entire length of the studio. Its whitewashed wall was completely covered with paintings. Small and large, watercolors and oils, abstract and impressionist, each canvas hugged the wall and fought for space.

"Oh, Sasha!" cried Vannie. "You must have at least thirty painters here."

Sasha's eyes flashed brightly. "Thirty-four. But wait, I'm not finished." With both hands, he pulled at two ridges partly hidden by a large canvas. The wall came forward. Then he flung his arms out like an impresario —and two panels rolled back to reveal an underwall as resplendent as the first. There were four sliding double panels in all. Sasha ran the length of the gallery, pulling and flinging, uncovering his two-tiered collection of one hundred and fifty underground paintings.

Ken's eyes narrowed. "Extraordinary. I'd never believe such carpentry possible in the Soviet Union. You must have paid a high price for it."

There was an awkward moment as Sasha's lip twitched. Brushing a speck from his velvet jacket, he explained, "A friend of mine designs sets for the Moscow Art Theater." Ken smiled, and the moment passed.

Sasha hastened to join Vannie at the far end of the gallery. She had stopped to inspect a small impressionist canvas in oil, a smiling young girl in white with slightly closed eyes, leaning against a beige background.

"This is beautiful, Sasha. It's a Fontanova, isn't it? I've never seen it before."

"It isn't mine, actually. Michael Petrov lent it to me for the exhibition."

No matter who dropped this ordinary Russian name, a short, impressed silence invariably followed. For Michael Petrov was one of a kind, moving with chameleon grace through Moscow's many social worlds. By profession, he was editor of a quarterly called *Amerikanskaya Zhizn*, an expensively produced distortion of American life. But even Soviet officials of nominally higher station deferred to him in a manner which the magazine alone could never explain.

"Sasha, does Michael Petrov want to sell the Fontanova? Is that why he's showing it here?"

"Ask him yourself, Vannie. He should be here any minute. . . . But wait, let me get you something to drink. Stay right here."

As Sasha scampered down the stairs, the studio door burst open. The first guests, bundled in overcoats, rushed forward to embrace him in a flourish of bear hugs. As coats and fur hats dropped on empty chairs, Sasha quickly folded back a Spanish screen in the corner, disclosing an oblong table laden with bottles and brimming glasses of vodka, the yellow herb-tinted *pertsovka*, and Soviet champagne. A second wave of guests burst in, and then a third. Old friends of Sasha's carried trays of canapés in from the kitchen, helping themselves to fresh caviar and rare radishes before passing them on. The studio soon filled up, and the scent of onions and black tobacco reached Vannie up on the balustrade.

Vannie was delighted by the spectacle below. For painters, Sasha's party was a marketplace to sell their art for illegal dollars. For foreign diplomats, it was a rare contact with nonofficial Russians. For Russian political dissenters, the noisy party was a secret news forum—a place to pass on quickly and quietly the news events rarely reported in the Soviet press: arrests, interrogations, trials, protest petitions. Vannie watched knowingly as, under the guise of effusive greetings and the rising

swells of cocktail patter, a variety of future, more inti-
mate meetings were being discreetly arranged. She ig-
nored the anonymous young men in black serge suits
who meandered around the studio with concentrated
indifference, sampling the conversation on behalf of the
KGB. The only informer Vannie recognized was Vladimir Maronov, who dabbled in collages with manicured
nails and reported on his artist friends with notorious
regularity.

As the guests flowed up to the gallery, Vannie spotted
Eric Fields steering his wife, Sally, up the stairs, a tentative hand under her elbow. Eric, a British exchange
student, led with his square-cut chin as if determined to
maintain civilized standards even in the wilds of Mus-
covy. His golden-skinned bride from South Carolina cast
two tenacious green eyes around the studio. She might
have seemed aggressive had not her vague smile revealed
two delicate dimples.

"Sally Fields," called Vannie, squeezing herself along
the balustrade toward the top of the staircase. "Why
didn't you two show up for lunch last week? I left the
invitation at the British embassy mailroom and you
didn't even call."

"I'm very sorry," Eric said. "We were terribly busy
last week."

"You mean you only have time for your secret Russian
friends," Vannie teased.

"Don't exaggerate," Sally said. "Eric simply forgot to
pick up our mail. Do invite us again."

"I will, but you two lead such exciting lives, you might be bored. . . ."

Neither of them was listening. Eric had turned to examine the sliding panels, and Sally had begun to chat with Maronov about collages. In the crowd of faces down below, Vannie recognized the sharply trimmed beard and tinted glasses of Michael Petrov. She quickly made her way down through the crush on the staircase.

Petrov was pleased that Vannie liked his Fontanova. Despite his frequent paeans to Soviet culture, he enjoyed Western approval of his artistic taste as much as he did the narrow-cut Italian suits and British sports cars that he somehow managed to import into the Soviet Union.

"If you're ever short of cash, Michael," Vannie offered, "let me know. I'll buy the painting from you."

He was amused. "Maybe I'll give it to you someday. As a farewell present."

"We're not leaving yet. But I'd really be happy to buy it, if it's not too expensive."

"Russians don't sell the things they love—they give them away. Haven't you learned that much about our country yet?"

As Vannie searched for a reply, Mario Campini, the personal secretary to the Italian ambassador, threw an arm around Petrov's broad shoulder. "Tovarich, tovarich, I see you've been to my Roman tailor."

Petrov gently shook off his arm. He liked Mario but resented the mocking "tovarich."

"*Ciao*, amico," Michael said. "How's the poem coming?"

"Slowly, slowly," Mario lamented. "Maybe I finish it in time for the hundredth anniversary of your great revolution."

Vannie smiled. "How do you find time to write poetry? Aren't you at the embassy all day?"

"Sì, signora. That's when I sleep and my colleagues don't even notice. So in the evening, when I go to my little private room at the Hotel Rossiya, I am fresh for my writing."

Grasping fingers pulled Vannie's hand to a moist mouth. Bernard Fauvet, the fastest hand kisser of the diplomatic set, bowed before her.

"What brings you here, Bernard? I wouldn't think you like modern painting."

He winked. "You are a very perceptive girl. These modern dribbles are rather crude for my taste, but these icons"—he breathed deeply—"*magnifique*." He drew her away from Mario and Petrov. "Tell me," he whispered confidentially, "who are all these other Russians?"

"Mostly painters," Vannie replied.

"And that blond girl, there, in the red sweater?"

"She translates for Interpresse, the Belgian news service. Ludmilla Rafaelovna something—I don't know her last name. . . . Excuse me, Bernard, but some good friends have just come in."

It was then that Vannie saw Lydia and Yuri entering the studio. She was surprised. Last night at the ballet, Lydia had given no hint that she might come, let alone bring Yuri.

Vannie took a step forward, then remembered her rule

19

of never greeting Russian friends till they first acknowl-
edged her. She retreated quickly toward the studio window. Would they want to greet her publicly, she
wondered—the usual kiss on both cheeks in front of so
many strangers? Vannie felt a strong hand on her shoulder. She turned. Yuri's handsome face with its high,
broad cheekbones was flushed as he leaned down to kiss
her cheek.

"Where are you running, Vannie? You are the only
one I know at this party, since Lydia has just deserted
me."

"I'm sorry, Yuri. I thought you might not want to be
seen with me."

"You foreigners are strange. You come to Russia to
know Russians—and then you run away when we need
you. Are you ashamed of us?"

"Oh, no, Yuri. It's just that friendships between Russians and Americans are officially discouraged. I don't
want to get you into trouble."

"But why are *you* so intimidated by what officials
think? There is no law in the Soviet Union forbidding us
to be friends. And if there were, I would break it."

"Vannie, Vannie, you naughty girl, you never told me
you knew Yuri Zhalkov." Bernard Fauvet, his face beam-
ing with discovery, grabbed Yuri's hand in both of his. "I
am delighted to make your acquaintance."

Yuri's face went pale. "How do you know my name? I
don't know you."

"Fauvet, I'm the chargé d'affaires of the Swiss embassy.
I knew you the minute you walked in. Family resem-

blance, of course. I thought you might be General Zhalkov's son, but Mike Petrov just told me you are his nephew. Your uncle was a frequent visitor at our embassy. He enjoyed playing chess with our former ambassador. Unfortunately, the general no longer comes to our receptions. We regard it as a great loss."

"A great loss," Yuri repeated numbly, then slowly took out a cigarette and lit it.

"But then," Fauvet continued, unperturbed by Yuri's reticence, "I suppose the general is busy these days with more important matters. When you see him, please convey my best wishes."

"I haven't seen my uncle in several months."

"Ah, pity. Do you work here in Moscow?"

"Occasionally."

"Fine, then. Perhaps you can continue the family tradition. We are giving a dinner Tuesday night, and several of your uncle's Army colleagues should be there. I shall send you an invitation through Mrs. Tomkins." With a paternal pat on Yuri's unresponding shoulder and a wink of complicity to Vannie, he left them.

"Is he a friend of yours, Vannie?" asked Yuri quietly.

"God, no, he's just a preening peacock. I didn't set him on to you, Yuri. I didn't even know your last name was Zhalkov."

"He said Petrov knew who I was. Which one is Petrov?"

"There, by the couch, with the beard. Fauvet's going over to him now. You don't know him?"

21

"Only by reputation, Vannie. That's enough to keep me away...."

"Stop gossiping, you two, I'm eavesdropping." With a dimpled hand extended to Yuri, Sally Fields smiled, certain that she should inspire a glint of recognition.

Yuri took her hand and held it. "Yes, we did meet . . . but I don't remember...."

"At Studentski Dom, Russian New Year's. But you never did tell me your name."

"Yuri Zhalkov," Vannie volunteered. "He's a geologist from Leningrad."

"What luck!" Sally's eyes lit up like a flash fire. "I hope to be in Leningrad next weekend. Will you be back there by then?"

Yuri dropped Sally's hand. "I'm not sure. I may still be in Moscow."

"Well, perhaps you'll return while I'm still there. I know so few people to guide me around." Sally withdrew a white card and a gold pencil from her purse. She printed quickly in Russian. "Here." She handed the card to Yuri. "If you should be in Leningrad before the end of April, please call. You do know the Hotel Sovietskaya." Yuri nodded and pocketed the card.

Vannie clutched a passing Eric Fields by the sleeve. "Yuri, this is Sally's husband. He's doing his thesis on the wartime siege of Leningrad, aren't you, Eric?"

Yuri asked Eric whom they would see in Leningrad, and the two men began conversing in an elegant Russian. Sally whispered to Vannie, "He's very attractive, your friend. Why don't you ask him to join us for tea at your place?"

Vannie hesitated. She had never invited Lydia or Yuri into the closely watched compound. But, swept up by Sally's insouciance, she responded, "Why not? How about Friday—say around five?"

"That would be lovely. You're an angel." Sally blew her a kiss and sailed away.

Vannie listened to Yuri and Eric, strangers a moment earlier, now happily discussing Russian history on the same wavelength. She felt like a hostess at the high pitch of her party. Then, as if a shadow had fallen, she looked up at the gallery. Commanding a full view of the studio, Vladimir Maronov's field of vision had narrowed down to Yuri and Eric. *Damned fink*, thought Vannie, *he's just ruined my party.*

Vannie looked for Lydia—and saw her standing beside Ken at the studio window, gazing down at the Wonder Wheel in Gorki Park below. She was a wisp of a girl, with fine dark hair braided in a gentle circle pinned loosely at the nape of her neck. Her hands belied her frailty, with broad palms and graying fingers coarsened by clay. She was startled by Vannie's touch on her shoulder.

"It's you, *dorogaya*." She seemed relieved. "Ken was just asking me to cast your head in bronze."

Vannie was surprised. "But you aren't even finished with the clay model."

"I should be by the time Ken gets back from Rome."

23

Lydia smiled assuringly. "Come by early this week. Maybe we can get in two sittings."

"Maybe tomorrow. Ken's plane leaves early, and after that I'm free."

Ken took Vannie's arm. "But that's tomorrow, and tonight there's still my packing to be done. Let's get started."

It took them ten minutes to leave the dimming studio, making their way among the flushed faces darkened by early evening shadows. There were kisses, handshakes, waves to the gallery. "Thank you, Sasha, it was unforgettable. . . . See you Friday, Sally. . . . Remember me, Michael, if you decide to sell the Fontanova. . . . Goodbye. . . . *au revoir* . . . *do svidanya*." By the time they left, Yuri and Lydia had already gone.

Outside, it had started to snow. "Oops, I forgot my shopping bag." Ken waited on the street as Vannie took the elevator back up to Sasha's. She found her things behind the kitchen door.

"Did you forget something, my dear?" It was Simone Durand.

"I'm always forgetting something." Vannie smiled as she pulled on her boots and dropped her shoes into the shopping bag. "It was very nice meeting you, Madame Durand. How long will you be in Moscow?"

"Just another week."

Vannie shook her hand. "Well, call if you are free for a drink. 'Bye again."

They found a taxi at the corner and rode back to the compound in silence. Entering the apartment, Ken made straight for the refrigerator. "Vodka is fine, but milk is healthier."

Vannie threw her shopping bag on the foyer chair. "You didn't enjoy it, did you? A party like that is so unusual."

"Unusual, but not very unofficial," came Ken's comment from the kitchen.

"Look, there's no way of giving a party in Moscow without inviting Maronov and Michael Petrov. But that Simone Durand was fascinating. Imagine, living ten years in Moscow and starting an entire school of modern painters." Vannie sat down and pulled off her boots.

"Sure, she's fascinating," said Ken, coming back into the foyer. "She spent those same ten years in Moscow living with a Soviet officer. I wonder which kind, Army or KGB. . . ."

"Before you wonder too far," Vannie snapped, "please tell me why you have to throw your old newspapers in my shopping bag." A copy of *Literaturnaya Gazeta* had slipped out of her bag onto the floor.

"That's not mine. I didn't . . ."

They both saw the single sheet of onionskin paper sticking out from behind the front page. Ken bent down and picked it up. It was typewritten, single-spaced, in Russian. He read it slowly, folded it carefully, and put it in his breast pocket.

Vannie had learned long ago that important stories came to Ken on just such typewritten sheets of onionskin paper. Unpublished news, petitions, documents, and protest letters were duplicated surreptitiously from typewriter to typewriter and passed secretly from hand to hand. The whispered Russian word for this underground "news service" was *samizdat*.

"I'll be back soon," Ken said. Nothing more. Vannie did not question him in the apartment because of the microphones concealed in the walls. She was asleep by the time he returned that night.

Early the next morning, Ken packed his own suitcase and left for Rome. When Vannie awoke, she found his note propped up on the telephone saying that he would call if, as they suspected, he was being reassigned. He left no explanation of the onionskin paper he had taken with him.

Chapter Two

The metal lid of the mail slot snapped shut. Vannie, still wearing a blue silk dressing gown, ran to the foyer to retrieve the thick white envelope which had been thrust through the slash in the front door. It contained a note from Bernard Fauvet, asking Vannie to deliver an enclosed dinner invitation to Yuri Zhalkov. She could pass it on this afternoon. Vannie had decided to go to Lydia's studio at three, when Yuri would be there.

Outside, the midday drizzle seemed to penetrate the double windows still sealed against the winter frost, drenching the yellow bedroom curtains in a limpid grayness. Vannie spied two fat roaches hanging in the folds. She was impatient—with the roaches, with the endless on-and-off Moscow thaw, with the hour that remained until three o'clock. Armed with her house slipper, she swiftly mashed two crunchy brown spines into the diaphanous yellow linen.

Disappointed that Fauvet had not invited her to dinner with Yuri—less because of the social slight than because she might be missing something—she withdrew her own collection of official invitations from her night table. Sitting on the edge of the bed, she slowly fingered the invitations, finding the embossed, gold-crested cards seductive to the touch. She counted five invitations, including lunch at the Italian ambassador's country dacha on Thursday.

The ambiance of diplomatic receptions excited Vannie. She relished the subtle variations of small talk, the casual dissimulation of covert glances, the carnal fragrance of intrigue. In Moscow, Vannie had finally found a life which matched her inner life in ambiguous intensity.

Until Ken's assignment to Russia nearly two years ago, Vannie had felt—whether with her family in Binghamton or with Ken for three years in Washington—that she was drifting and meandering through schools, people, jobs, in a life that somehow wasn't hers. She had once confessed to Ken that "my life has been just one long nothing" since the death of her Russian grandfather. It was through this elegantly dressed patriarch, who had hardly learned English, that she heard about the almond-eyed, auburn-tressed grandmother she most resembled, who had died in Kiev during the Russian Civil War, and of how her grandfather had dodged the Reds and slipped through the White lines with a baby daughter, Vannie's mother.

"I was the only one in the family interested in those stories. Everyone else was being one hundred percent American. I can't speak Russian anymore, but I still understand a little. I was only thirteen when he died, but his death left me in some sort of lurch. In some way, deep inside of me, I've never been attached to anything ever since."

When Ken was assigned to Moscow, Vannie rushed out and bought three grammars, Pares' *History of Russia*, Massie's *Nicholas and Alexandra*, a two-volume Russian dictionary, and an even heavier set of Russian language records. She immersed herself in Cyrillic calligraphy and Slavic sibilants until, at last, the Aeroflot Ilyushin set them down at Moscow's Sheremetyevo Airport.

The birches, pines, and firs along the road from the airport swayed gently in the faint summer breeze. But the barren ugliness of Moscow itself was shocking—a dusty, naked city of ill-fitted housing and ill-tempered people. Eight and ten-lane boulevards ringed and crossed the sprawling city, bearing odd trucks, trolleybuses, taxis, and a few rumbling passenger cars. Broad sidewalks isolated silent pedestrians. Squat old women in long black skirts swept the streets with brooms of birch twigs. Where, Vannie wondered, were the swaggering Cossacks of yesteryear?

It was relatively easy for a foreigner, once admitted, to settle in Moscow—if he had enough dollars. The official "special services" organization for foreign residents, called UPDK, provided the Tomkinses with a compact three-room apartment and Ken with a snug two-room office. Around the corner from their compound, the exclusive hard-currency supermarket offered Russian beef, fresh caviar dolloped out of twenty-pound tins, untaxed

Johnnie Walker (Red and Black labels), pale oranges from Algeria, and bright bulging tomatoes from Bulgaria. Such luxuries were paid for in *talonchiki,* multicolored coupons resembling Monopoly money, which were issued in rectangular gray booklets by the Soviet State Bank in exchange for Western currency.

An occasional foray into ordinary Russian shops— whose meager shelves were stacked with bags of salt, sugar, and flour, dusty tins of smoked fish, and clusters of dried-out sausages—persuaded most foreigners of their privileged position in the UPDK world of special services. A single ride in a Soviet trolleybus, with its shoving of shoulders and protrusion of bellies, chased most diplomats' wives back to the privacy of their own cars.

The ubiquitous UPDK provided Ken with a secretary and driver. The organization also provided cleaning maids, Russian-language teachers, ballet instructors, tennis coaches, even a breeding mate for a lonely dog. So enveloped was Vannie by the services of the Soviet authorities that it was months before she realized that, despite much hectic motion back and forth, all the Russians she knew had been officially chosen for her.

Most of the two thousand Westerners in Moscow spent most of their time with one another. They met amid the charred garbage heaps and discarded transport crates of the compound courtyard. They exchanged gossip while queuing up to buy, and then to pay, in the dollar supermarket. Evenings, they tinkled iced cocktails in interchangeable living rooms of Scandinavian teak. Where, oh where, Vannie sighed, was Russia?

After Vannie had toured the Kremlin churches and palaces, Ken's secretary showed her the art museums, the Pushkin and the Tretyakov. Then there were the literary houses: Tolstoy and Gorki. Within the twenty-five-mile radius of Moscow, beyond which resident foreigners were forbidden to travel without special permission, a half-dozen mansions built by the czarist aristocracy waited forlornly to be inspected.

When Ken was free in the evening, they went to the Bolshoi Theater to see *Boris Godunov*, to the Kremlin Palace of Congresses to watch *Swan Lake*, to the old Moscow Conservatory to hear Rostropovich conduct Shostakovich. But after four months in Moscow, Vannie still felt like an outsider. After the theater, the Russians would stampede to the cloakroom, jostle each other to the doors, and disappear into the buses and down the subway kiosks. Vannie and Ken would drive home alone in their sleek black Chevrolet Impala.

Moscow came alive for Vannie only in winter. That first November, when the sharp east wind blew away the flabby clouds of autumn, she ventured out again—this time on foot. The snow had covered the empty lots, decorated the boulevards, sprinkled the fur hats, and cloaked the muddy Moscow River in a smoky white patina. As the primeval Russian snows blanketed the Communist city, endowing grim streets with landscape and crude peasants with pungence, Vannie found the most ordinary activities of singular moment: bargaining for tomatoes at the collective-farm market with sleepy-eyed Uzbeks, skiing across the frozen, windswept river to

31

reach warm sanctuary in a patch of evergreens, swimming through the fog of a heated outdoor pool to glimpse the golden Kremlin domes revealed in a sudden gust of wind.

Once Vannie picked up the language, she plunged into chance conversations with Russians, regarding each as a dramatic adventure, later transforming them into amusing anecdotes. It was in the Impressionist Room of the Pushkin Museum that she met Lydia Chernova sketching Van Gogh's "Prisoners at Exercise," and through Lydia, Vannie discovered the underground artists of Moscow. Their cramped studios were often a stone's throw from the Kremlin, but their canvases were closer to Greenwich Village and Montmartre than to the tractor heroines of "socialist realism."

Lydia had brought her only to the first studio. After sipping tea from steamy glasses and vodka from chipped cups, it was the painter himself who offered to take Vannie to another studio a week later. There she met someone to take her to the third. So it went, like a relay system. Arrangements were made there and then, and invariably kept. There were no reminders, because the artists knew that all foreigners' phones, and many of their own, were tapped by the KGB.

None of the underground artists' studios resembled the luxurious appointments of Sasha Rabichov. Some of them were neat and spare—a cot, a table, two straight chairs, a bare swept floor, perhaps a small icon nailed to an empty wall. When a foreigner entered, the unfinished canvas was turned discreetly inward on the easel and a paper shade placed over a weak bulb. Other studios were cluttered—last night's glasses sticking to a soiled oilcloth, a slab of bread and beady cheese resting forlornly on the windowsill. Sometimes a girlfriend, who had forgotten to leave, sat cross-legged on a gristly rug, guzzling vodka from the spout of a greasy kettle.

Vannie would admire the paintings and listen attentively to the gossip, nodding with compassion to the tale of a writer harassed by censors or a painter burning out his talent in vodka. The artists liked Vannie and thought her discreet.

To a few artists, Vannie had returned often, simply dropping by to pass a lonely afternoon when Ken was on some official tour of a far-off Soviet province. During the long summer and autumn of 1968, when Ken worked in Czechoslovakia, Vannie would often spend whole days in Moscow going from one artist to another, allaying her hunger with a butter roll and a glass of kvass bought for a few kopecks from a street vendor. She rode the subway and buses or walked to the artists' studios because the huge American car, with its specially numbered license plates, would have compromised her friends.

Twice that second winter, Vannie had summoned up the courage to buy an abstract painting, as fearful of her taste as of the illicit transaction. The underground paintings, regarded by the authorities as "bourgeois" and "decadent," were permitted neither public exhibition in Russia nor an export stamp to be shown abroad. Officially, they were non-art executed by non-persons. Each time Vannie had bought a painting, she and the artist had carefully masked the "subversive" canvas with old copies of *Pravda* and bits of string. Each time she had taken the canvas home by taxi after dark and, even before removing her coat, locked the painting in her steamer trunk. Neither artist had asked how she would ever get the painting out of Russia. Vannie herself, in her exuberance, had given it no serious thought. Perhaps Lydia might give her some advice this afternoon.

For most of her forays into the Russian world, Vannie purposely dressed in an old cloth coat and tatty fur hat, hoping to slip through the cultural lines unobtrusively. For this afternoon's sitting at Lydia's, she slipped out of her Paris dressing gown into a moss-green skirt with a matching round-necked sweater, for Lydia found bright colors and fussy lines distracting.

When she finished dressing, Vannie wrote a short note to Eric and Sally Fields, reminding them of Friday tea and assuring them that Yuri would be there. She slipped the note into an envelope and placed it, along with Fauvet's invitation, in the side pocket of her purse. She would drop off the note to the Fieldses on the way home from Lydia's.

As Vannie walked along the roadway leading out of the compound, the phone in the sentry box rang, breaking the silence of the courtyard. Two pairs of eyes surveyed her from inside the wooden booth. She knew the militiamen were jotting down her name and time of departure. But Vannie now accepted this record of her comings and goings as routinely as she did the roaches crawling up the pipes.

Lydia's basement studio off the Arbat was only five blocks away. But, once on the Arbat, Vannie felt that she had left the guarded, circumscribed life of the transient foreign colony and entered the real and rooted world of Muscovites. The narrow Arbat, with its crowded four- and five-story tenements, had once been crammed with lively pushcarts and open stalls. Now, with state stores half-concealing their faded wares through grime-streaked windows, the Arbat had become a street of nostalgia. Its very memories of prerevolutionary Moscow had attracted many of the artists whose studios Vannie visited.

Vannie turned off the Arbat. How complicated it had been the first time she came to Lydia's more than a year ago: halfway down the street, across an empty lot, up a wooden plank, through a shoddy courtyard to the last door on the left. Then down a flight of wooden stairs to the rusty iron door at the right of the wall telephone— the door was always open—and then straight to the end of the corridor. She had got lost. When she finally found the correct courtyard door, she had tripped on the warped stairs and cut her knee on a stray pipe. She had burst into the studio an hour late. Lydia, calmly working with her clay, had been mystified by Vannie's profuse apologies. "An hour isn't a very long time. You shouldn't have rushed so. Here, let me wash your knee." She had offered Vannie strong coffee and halvah. Both ate and drank until the fading ray of light, through the sole barred window, closed the basement room into darkness.

Vannie had felt at peace. Had it been Lydia's calm presence, the quiet order of her studio, or the luxury of an afternoon away from watchful eyes?

This time, the iron door at the bottom of the stairs was closed. Vannie knocked. There was no answer. She turned the knob. The door was locked. She knocked again, stronger. Then she heard footsteps in the corridor. A key turned.

"It's only me, Vannie," she said. The door slowly opened. Yuri stood silently behind the threshold. Beside him, a short, middle-aged man with a pale, flat face and sharp nose regarded her with curious amusement. Yuri gave no sign of whether she should stay or go.

"Come in." The pale man beckoned. Vannie entered. The door closed behind her, and the three of them walked single file down the corridor. A yellowish bulb illuminated the toilet on their right. At the door to Lydia's studio, Vannie paused. The stranger reached past her head and threw open the door.

Vannie gasped when she saw the studio. Had there been an explosion? Broken ceramic and plaster were strewn on the floor. The high shelves opposite the door were empty. The fragile sculpture—the delicately cast faces that Lydia had created during a decade of work—lay smashed below. Vannie's own clay head had been cut down the center, the bruised halves lying facedown beside the pedestal on which Lydia had molded it. Lydia was crouched in a corner, staring into space, her mouth open, numb with shock.

Vannie stepped tentatively into the room, broken

ceramic splintering beneath her feet. She nearly brushed against two unshaven young thugs, slouched against the wall. One of them held a thick metal chain. She pulled her arm back as if burned.

The corner table, once covered with Yuri's collection of semiprecious stones, had been swept clean. Behind the table, a fat, bald man with round, rimless glasses, wearing a loose-fitting brown suit, sat hovering over a small, lined copybook, a black fountain pen in his left hand.

Frightened, Vannie retreated, but the pale man barred the door. "If you've come to see your friends, why don't you say hello?"

"No, I mustn't stay. This is none of my business."

"Let her go," said Yuri. "She has nothing to do with it."

"That I will decide, Zhalkov," said the fat man, mopping his bald head with a rumpled gray handkerchief.

"Just as you decided to break the sculpture," Yuri snapped.

"We have a written warrant to search everything in the studio. That includes the inside of the sculpture," the fat man declared. "Tomorrow you can file a complaint. At the moment, I am interested in your friend." He started to write. "Your name, please, and the purpose of your visit."

"Why should I tell you?" Vannie asked defiantly. "Who are you?"

The fat man sat motionless for a moment, then put down the fountain pen and produced a thick, plastic wallet, flipping it open to a card with the large Russian letters KGB. "Kovalov, Sergei Andreyevich, captain investigator, Committee on State Security," he said. Pointing to the pale man with the sharp nose: "My assistant, Sergeant Valentin Steklov." Then smiling amiably at the two thugs: "Comrades Popov and Smirnov—official witnesses to the search." Popov, who was twirling the chain, smirked, baring brown chipped teeth.

Vannie shuddered. *Oh, God, what have I got into?*

"Your name, please, and the purpose of your visit," Captain Kovalov repeated.

Vannie glanced imploringly at Yuri, who remained impassive. Finally, she said: "My name's Vannie. I pose for my friend Lydia. I was just dropping by."

"Your identity papers, please."

Vannie clutched her bag. *If they know you're the wife of an American correspondent, you are going to get everyone into trouble.* "I have none."

"Look inside your bag. All Soviet citizens must carry identity papers. It is the law. If not, you are punishable by arrest."

"No, you can't arrest me. I'm an American. I just don't have my passport with me. No one ever told me. . . ."

"Ah." Kovalov smiled broadly. "You are a foreigner? And you are a friend of Lydia Chernova and Yuri Zhalkov. How cozy."

"Valya," he snapped, "go out and telephone the Foreign Ministry. Ask Alexei to check the American file for a Mrs. Vanny."

"Why must you check it?" Vannie's voice was shrill.

Kovalov resumed writing in his copybook as Valya left the room.

Vannie ran to the door. "Wait. Don't telephone."

Valya returned, pushing her back into the room. "You stay here."

"But that's not my whole name. It's Tomkins. Vannie Tomkins."

The two Russians exchanged looks. Valya went out into the corridor again, leaving the door ajar.

"When he comes back . . . may I leave then?"

Kovalov nodded.

"All right. Then I'll wait for him in the corridor." She dashed across the room. The two thugs lunged forward to grab her; Kovalov waved them back with a flick of his pen. Then he rose slowly and followed her into the dimly lit corridor, closing the door behind him.

"I'm staying here," she said defensively. "I'm not going back into that room."

He raised his eyebrows. "But they are your friends, Mrs. Tomkins."

"That's just it. I can't bear to look at Lydia and all that broken sculpture."

"Yes, that's too bad," he said. "You know them both for a long time?"

Vannie nodded.

"Have you many friends among the Soviet people, Mrs. Tomkins?"

"A few," Vannie admitted cautiously.

"And the general, Zhalkov's uncle? Is he also a friend?"

"No. But I heard about him. He likes to play chess, doesn't he?"

"You claim he is not a friend, but you know his hobbies."

The KGB captain was amused; foreigners' lies were so transparent. "But surely you were introduced to General Zhalkov. He often met foreigners at embassy receptions. The Swiss perhaps. Or the Italian?"

"No. Well, maybe. I don't remember. One meets so many people at receptions." Vannie hoped she had impressed him.

"Surely your friend Yuri has told you about him. He was very proud of his uncle."

"Even if he did . . . what has that to do with me?"

"That, Mrs. Tomkins, we intend to find out. Sooner or later."

Valya entered the corridor. "Alexei said to hold her until he gets here."

Kovalov opened the door to the studio. "Come back inside, Mrs. Tomkins, if you wish to leave this afternoon," he said evenly. Reluctantly, Vannie reentered the room. No one inside had moved.

"Yuri," Vannie whispered as she moved past him, "what are they looking for?"

He reflected. "Proof."

"Of what?"

"Of how my uncle died," he said.

"Silence, Zhalkov!" Kovalov bellowed. "This is an affair of state. She is a foreigner."

40

"You should have thought of that before you insisted she stay," Yuri replied. He pulled up a chair for Vannie and then crossed the room to Lydia. He smoothed back the strand of hair that had fallen across her forehead. Nodding almost imperceptibly, Lydia straightened herself up, then slowly walked over to her tea things, the only objects in the room left undisturbed. She lit the small primus stove, standing motionless until the kettle whistled. She fixed a cup of tea and brought it to Vannie, who took the steaming cup with one hand and, with the other, pressed Lydia's palm against her cheek.

There was an impatient knock on the front door. Valya went out to the corridor, returning a moment later with a fastidiously groomed young Soviet official. The stranger removed his tweed topcoat and automatically handed it to Valya. A blue handkerchief in his breast pocket, matching an impeccably knotted paisley tie, announced his rank of privilege. He inspected the room with quick, measured glances. Pavel Ivanovich Romanov, representative of the Ministry of Foreign Affairs, did not enjoy the untidy conditions of a KGB search.

"You are Vanessa Tomkins," he said. "Your husband is the correspondent of Capitol Radio Corporation. He is now in Rome." Romanov spoke English without accent.

"Has she been searched yet?" he asked the KGB captain in Russian.

"But I have nothing on me," Vannie protested. She opened her handbag so that he could see that she was not lying. He looked inside. "And these letters?"

Yuri stepped forward. "Under Soviet law, you are not

allowed to search her bag without a representative of her embassy present."

"Perfectly correct, Zhalkov," Romanov answered. "But it will not be necessary to search her handbag. Mrs. Tomkins has nothing to hide. If they are innocent letters, she will let me see them herself."

Vannie held the two envelopes in her hand. "They're just two invitations. Of no importance, really."

"I will be an excellent judge," he said, plucking the envelopes from her hand. Neither Fauvet's invitation to Yuri nor Vannie's to the Fieldses was sealed.

The Foreign Ministry official read them rapidly. Then he translated them aloud into Russian at dictation speed, for Captain Kovalov to transcribe into his copybook.

"Tell me, Mrs. Tomkins," Romanov then asked, "why are you transmitting an invitation from the Swiss embassy to Yuri Zhalkov?"

"The chargé d'affaires didn't know Yuri's address."

"But he knew that you did."

"Well, yes. He just assumed it."

"Why should he have assumed it?"

"I don't know. I suppose because we're friends."

"Do you possess other communications for Yuri Zhalkov?"

"No. Why should I? It was just that. . . ."

"But," he persisted, "any communication you received for Yuri Zhalkov . . . or from him, you would, of course, deliver."

"Yes, I suppose . . . but. . . ."

"Vannie," said Yuri evenly, "you are under no obligation to answer any questions besides your name and address."

"Mind your business, Zhalkov. I am sure Mrs. Tomkins is aware of her rights."

"No, I'm not. I want to leave. Do you have any right to keep me?"

The Foreign Ministry official smiled, a brief softening of the jawline. "We shall only detain you a few minutes longer. First tell us why you are arranging a tea for Mr. and Mrs. Fields with your friend Zhalkov."

"Don't make it sound so important. I just thought it would be nice to bring them together."

"Nice? Curious word. Surely you had a more specific purpose?"

She reflected. Then, believing that the simple truth would vindicate her: "I thought Yuri would be able to tell the Fieldses things about Leningrad that they wouldn't find in the guidebooks. It's his city, and the Fieldses are foreigners."

"What did you imagine Zhalkov might tell Mr. and Mrs. Fields?"

Vannie was perplexed by the question. "If I knew what Yuri was going to tell the Fieldses, I could tell them myself. But I don't know Leningrad that well either."

"Mrs. Tomkins, let us not pretend that you are ignorant of Mr. Fields' activities."

"I am not pretending anything. Everybody knows that Eric Fields is an exchange student at Moscow University."

"Yes, he is enrolled at the university, Mrs. Tomkins. But he is, in fact, an agent of British Intelligence."

"That's not true. He's here on a legitimate cultural exchange program. Your ministry must have approved his visa."

"At a party yesterday," Romanov continued, "Mrs. Fields asked that you put her and her husband in touch with Yuri Zhalkov."

"You mean when I spoke to her at Sasha Rabichov's? How do you know?" Then, realizing the naïveté of the question, she plunged further. "Mrs. Fields didn't ask me to arrange anything. I invited her and her husband to tea, and then she asked if I might invite Yuri Zhalkov too." Romanov repeated her words in Russian to Captain Kovalov.

Then, returning to Vannie, Romanov persisted, "And you agreed to lend your apartment for this meeting?"

"No, no. No one asked me to *lend* my apartment for anything. I volunteered." Romanov translated her words again in Russian for the KGB captain to transcribe into his copybook. With her words accurately echoed, Vannie was suddenly stunned; everything she had said incriminated her further.

"Is there anything more you wish to tell us?" Romanov asked solicitously.

"I . . ." she began. Then she shook her head. "No, nothing."

Romanov glanced down again at the two invitations still in his hand. "I'll keep the one for Zhalkov. Here, take the one for Mr. and Mrs. Fields." Vannie slipped the invitation back into her purse.

"You may go now, Mrs. Tomkins," he said, reaching for Kovalov's copybook. Flipping through the pages, he added: "I wish you a pleasant tea."

She had been dismissed, but now she hesitated. Why were the two thugs grinning at her? She crossed the room to Lydia, broken ceramic crunching under her feet. "I'll come back and sit for you again," she whispered, hoping these were words of comfort.

Yuri opened the door. Vannie shook his hand formally, avoiding his look of pity—or was it contempt? He closed the door quietly behind her.

She climbed slowly up the wooden staircase into the dark courtyard thick with cabbage smells. It was dinnertime. She leaned against the building façade, letting the cold stone and fresh air clear her head. She was free at last. But it brought little relief from the wincing pain; she had left her best Russian friends in the hands of the KGB.

Chapter Three

It was noon on Vannie's watch as the black Impala abruptly swung off the concrete six-lane boulevard onto the narrow tarmac bridge spanning the Moscow River. Ivan Fyodorovich, the driver, slowed down as they passed through the snow-tipped birch and spruce trees lining the country lanes of Serebreny Bar. He pulled the car up at the picket fence surrounding the Italian ambassador's green clapboard dacha. Vannie asked Ivan to come back for her at three.

Vannie had at first resolved to tell no one about the KGB search at Lydia's studio. In a few days' time, when the shock receded, the jumble of painful images might sort itself out. Then, she hoped, she would absorb the scene into her knowledge of things.

She fled from swimming pool to ballet class, seizing distractions, running trivial errands—dodging the sting of recollection. Twice a day she chopped up chunks of stale bread, flung the crumbs from the kitchen window, and watched the sparrows swoop down into the slush. For the evening receptions, she showered hastily, fussed with her green mascara, and plunged into the protective patter of diplomatic small talk. Staying a bit too long, drinking one brandy too many, she rode home in the frosty haze and sought the comfort of her feather quilt.

Yet each night alone, memory asserted its right, proffering its vivid details: the splintered ceramic crunching under foot, the "witness" swinging his chain, her sculpted head battered on the floor. Again she saw Lydia's numbed face, heard Yuri's steely warning: *"They have no right to search you."* Cruelest of all, the two invitations lying so meekly in her handbag—why had she surrendered them so easily?

By Wednesday night Vannie could no longer contain her secret. She told the story, skipping names and omitting details, to her friend Nancy Colt, an archivist at the American embassy. Nancy advised her to avoid Soviet acquaintances until Ken's return. The incident might have consequences, she warned. She offered Vannie two Valiums to calm her sleep. And Thursday morning, half-waking, Vannie replayed her role: She firmly refused to open her handbag and courageously defended her friends. Upon rising, Vannie was determined to return to Lydia's studio.

Yet she did not return. If Lydia and Yuri had already been arrested, she reasoned with her morning coffee, it would be an empty gesture. And if they were still there, a return visit might compromise them further. She decided to telephone. She dialed their number and let it ring a dozen times. When no one answered, she hung up, at first relieved—and then chagrined.

What did Nancy mean by consequences, Vannie brooded. Would the authorities force them to leave Rus-

sia? Trunks packed quickly; good-byes—forever. And
her paintings: It would be too late to take them with her.
The customs inspectors would turn the trunk upside
down hoping to uncover a rolled-up canvas of "smug-
gled" underground art.

All because she had been an innocent bystander at a
KGB search. But Vannie sensed she might be more than
a bystander. *"Would you deliver to Yuri Zhalkov any
communications you received for him?"* the Foreign
Ministry man had asked. Those two invitations—
Fauvet's and the Fieldses' (did Eric really work for MI-
5?). The KGB captain had smirked when she denied
having known General Zhalkov. Had she indeed met him
at some embassy reception? At the Italians' last October?

Ken might remember. But if she telephoned him, she
could hardly ask about her paintings, let alone mention
the name of General Zhalkov. *"This is an affair of state."*

Vannie had been invited to the Italian ambassador's
for lunch at one o'clock. According to Ken, Federico
Succioli, who had been schooled by the Jesuits, possessed
the keenest political mind in Moscow. Vannie decided to
arrive early.

On the clean-swept porch of the Italian dacha, she
stamped off the wet snow clinging to her boots and
knocked. The curtains were still drawn. Perhaps no one
had arrived; lunch was usually cooked at the Moscow
residence and brought out to the dacha in heated con-
tainers. Finally, the white-frocked Spanish butler opened
the door.

"The ambassador and Madame Succioli have gone for

a walk. They should be back shortly. Will you come in and wait?"

Vannie glanced in at the cedar-paneled living room where the Succiolis gave the gayest parties in Moscow. Away from militiamen and cockroaches, amid crabmeat mousse and cases of champagne, a Ceylonese or Brazilian guitar-and-drum combo would play until four in the morning—rock-and-roll beat flinging arms and hips, releasing nervous energy in syncopated frenzy.

"No, thank you. I'll wander around and see if I can find them." Vannie preferred to speak to the ambassador in the open air.

She walked from the dacha toward the river, where on sunny Sundays in deep winter, families of cross-country skiers would glide over the ice. Old men chopped out holes to let down fishing lines. While waiting for a nibble under the cold sun, they built small fires on the ice to warm their hands. But now, between the seasons, before the rowboats came out and children jumped into the brown waters, there was nothing to do but walk in the gray quiet, avoiding the puddles of melting snow.

A hundred yards from the riverbank, Vannie made out the tall, graceful figures of the Succiolis. They could have appeared in *Vogue*—the Beautiful People jetting from Rome to Rio, Laura with her feline eyes, Federico with his broad shoulders and perpetual tan.

Vannie rushed forward. They were walking slowly, flanking Federico's private secretary, Mario Campini, their eyes cast down as if studying the rhythmic rise and fall of their suede boots with each step in the soft snow.

They did not see Vannie until she was a few yards away.

"I hope you don't mind my coming early, but our driver had to go to a meeting. Must be the chauffeurs' local of the KGB," she joked.

No one laughed. "I'm sorry," she apologized. "I've said something wrong."

Federico touched her arm. "No, Vannie. Forgive us. We find no humor in KGB jests today. But we are always glad to see you."

"I suppose I should have called before coming so early. I just thought. . . ." Then she noticed a stocky young man in a navy nylon raincoat standing twenty paces behind them.

"Come walk with me a bit, Vannie," Federico said, "and you'll soon understand." Mario and Laura paired off in front of them.

As Vannie took her first steps with the ambassador's arm linked in hers, the stocky Russian followed them, keeping his distance of twenty paces.

"He's following us!" Vannie announced.

"It would seem so."

"He can't do that!"

"Why not?" Federico was amused at her outrage. "They follow everyone in this country. Even each other."

"But not an ambassador—like this—so openly."

"Yes, I must admit the gremlin right behind us is a new touch. I know most of their ways of keeping tabs on me—I should after five years in Moscow. This may be their way of asking me to leave." Then the ambassador tightened his grip on Vannie's arm; they both stopped. "Look behind you," Federico commanded. "What is he doing?"

"He's stopped too. He's looking at the trees," Vannie said.

"Good, we have embarrassed him a little. Perhaps he is human after all." Federico walked on, turning up the collar of his camel's hair coat. "Come, Vannie, let us pay no more attention to him." As Vannie caught up, he asked, "Shall we take the shortcut to the dacha? Your feet must be wet."

"A little. But I came early to ask you a favor. It's rather important to me. Could you and Laura take out a couple of paintings for me next time you go to Rome?"

"That shouldn't be necessary, Vannie. You can take them out yourself. It's a matter of permission from the Tretyakov Gallery. Or is it the Ministry of Culture now?"

"But they're abstracts, which they rarely let out officially. With your diplomatic immunity, though, you might take them out fairly easily."

"So you want me to smuggle out abstract paintings?"

"It's not smuggling," Vannie protested. "I've paid for them. They're my legally owned paintings. In any other country, Federico. . . ."

"This is not any other country. Never for a moment permit yourself the luxury of living here as if it were." He paused. "We all do occasionally. That is our weakness."

"Then you won't take the paintings out?"

"I'm sorry, Vannie. At this moment, I cannot risk it. You do understand."

"You mean the gremlin behind us."

"Among other things." He took her arm again. "Vannie, unpleasant things have been happening in Moscow these last few weeks. At our embassy, too. Perhaps when they blow over. Ask me again in the fall."

"What kinds of things? Is there something special?"

"Every year since I've been here, Vannie, the trouble starts in March and reaches its peak in May. As regular as spring cleaning."

"What trouble?" Vannie implored.

Without losing his stride, the ambassador turned slightly. The gremlin was keeping his distance of twenty paces—too far back to overhear. "All right," Federico said. "But not a word to anyone." Vannie nodded.

"The Russians tried to blackmail Mario last night. He refused. He came to tell me this morning. I am now obliged to send him back to Rome."

"You don't believe him?"

"*Sì, sì*, of course I do. But it is not a matter of personal trust. Rome has already been informed. There are people in our Foreign Office who might already be wondering what kind of crazy diplomat writes poetry at the Hotel Rossiya at midnight. They may even suspect that the Russians succeeded in blackmailing Mario long ago. God help us if there were a leak in our embassy now."

"But it's unfair, sending him home," Vannie protested. "You're punishing him for telling you the truth. He would have been better off keeping it to himself."

53

"Perhaps. But then the Russians would have tried to blackmail him again. And again. And if they didn't succeed, they would force him out of the country on some other pretext. Accuse him of drunken driving, or not paying his rent at the Rossiya, or some other nonsense. No, it is better to send him home now, quietly. For him to stay on in Moscow would be very foolish."

"And this kind of thing happens every spring?"

"It may be more serious this year," the ambassador conceded. "It's too early to tell. We'll first have to see how the Zhalkov affair turns out."

"You mean the general?" Vannie exclaimed. The ambassador nodded.

"How do you know about him, Federico? Was he a friend of yours?"

"Not really," he said lightly. "I met him first in Rome years ago. He was stationed there as military attaché. Russians can sometimes be rather friendly when they're posted abroad."

"You must have been upset when he died."

The ambassador looked at her sharply, but he saw the remark was meant only as condolence. "Well, you know, friendship is quite another matter once the Russian returns to Moscow. General Zhalkov did come to our embassy reception last fall."

"Did I meet him?" Vannie interrupted.

The ambassador shrugged his shoulders. "Perhaps. You might have. But he didn't stay long. It was more a political gesture than a personal one. It was a month or so after the invasion of Czechoslovakia. I suspect he was rather . . . disturbed by it." And then in a low tone, almost to himself: "And now he has been assassinated."

"He's been *what?* Are you sure? Who told you?"

"It was on the Voice of America this morning. Why? Isn't that how you know of his death?"

"No, I don't listen to the radio. I . . . oh, Federico, I thought there was an obituary in the Russian papers—that's how you knew." She gripped his arm. "But who assassinated General Zhalkov?"

"Vannie dear," Laura called, "shall we go in for a drink now?"

"Please, Federico," Vannie whispered. "Not yet. I must tell you something."

"You and Mario go in now," Federico called back. "We'll join you in a few minutes." He steered her through a narrow footpath of firm snow leading from the road through a thicket of birch trees. "What's the matter, *cara?*"

"I walked in on a KGB search Monday at one of my Russian friends'. She's a sculptress and a friend of Yuri Zhalkov, the general's nephew. The KGB men asked me if I knew the general. One of them asked if I had met him at your embassy. Or maybe he asked if you knew him—I forget exactly. But they smashed my friend's sculpture. Yuri told me that they were looking for proof of his uncle's death. He didn't say murder."

"Perhaps it wasn't murder. The Russians sometimes let a fake story out to cover up the real story."

"But wouldn't they prefer the story of a natural death to cover up an assassination? Not the opposite?"

Federico shrugged his shoulders. "I suspect it's more complicated. According to the Voice of America, the assassination took place three months ago, shortly before Christmas. A captain in Zhalkov's command supposedly killed him. Now if it had really happened just like that, why didn't the Russians just put a small obituary in the papers announcing that Zhalkov had suffered a stroke, or 'died suddenly,' as they say so often? They've covered up murders that way before. And if he died in good grace, why wasn't there a state funeral? Instead, the first news of his death comes from abroad three months later. And because a captain killed him, we're all supposed to think there might be some Army plot."

"Then you don't believe the VOA story?"

The ambassador smiled. "Do you, Vannie?"

"Well, they may be right. He might have been assassinated. But if they found the murderer, why would they be questioning me, or even Yuri, about it?"

"So, Vannie, we both deduce that there's something fishy about the story. The next question we must ask is whose interest does the story serve. Hard to tell, since we don't even know how, or through whom, the story got out of Russia in the first place."

"Didn't the Voice of America give any source?"

"They quoted an unsigned article in the London *Banner* the day before. So the question is how the *Banner* got the story."

"Through a pigeon, probably."

"A what?"

Vannie laughed. "I'm sorry. That's American journal-

ists' slang for someone who takes a story or a letter out of
Moscow in his airline bag or hidden in his shoe."

"Does Ken do that?"

"Not often, but he'll sometimes take something out for
a friend."

"And where is Ken now?"

"Not in London." Vannie smiled. "He's meeting his
foreign editor in Rome."

The ambassador nodded. "Pity he didn't take your
paintings out in his suitcase."

Vannie shook her head. "They're too big, even rolled
up."

"Then you have little choice, Vannie." He patted her
arm. "You must try and get your paintings out through
official channels. You might get permission if the Zhalkov
affair doesn't get any bigger."

Through a gap in a cluster of pine trees, they glimpsed
the back of the dark-green dacha standing serenely in the
blanket of gray snow. In the clearing behind the house,
they crossed a patch of brown grass. "See," Vannie said,
digging her heel in the soft earth, "spring will come to
Russia. Someday."

"The eternal Russian promise," the ambassador said
as he opened the back door to the dacha.

In the living room, the first guests had arrived. After
the opening pleasantries, Vannie looked for Mario. She
found him at the bay window, staring wordlessly at the
gremlin pacing by the gate.

Chapter Four

In his small room on the seventh floor of the Hotel Rossiya overlooking the Kremlin, Mario Campini had sat alone the night before with his unfinished poem, staring down at the onion domes of St. Basil's Church with their crazy curlicues and wild colors.

They reminded him somehow of his young manhood, days of incoherent patterns and madly changing moods. He thought back to motorcycling on the Appian Way, with Claudia resting her face in the curve of his shoulders. During that time, he had written four novels and two books of criticism. But at forty, he had bowed to family convention, married a virgin from Bologna, and became a diplomat. Now he was private secretary to the ambassador in Moscow. He picked up his pen and crossed out a word.

A knock on the door. Luda entered, carrying a glass of tea in a silver-plated holder. The hotel bar and restaurant closed down at eleven o'clock. But, for a pair of stockings or a silk scarf at holiday time, Luda would fix him tea once or twice during the night, depending on how late he worked.

Luda was a *dejournaya*, one of the "dailies" posted on

each floor of every Soviet hotel. Her desk was positioned, as was customary, in the corridor opposite the stair, in full view of the elevator. As guests left in the morning for the day's sightseeing, they handed her their keys. Luda kept them in her top drawer. By midnight, when most of Moscow had closed down, she had usually returned the last key to the final returning tourist.

Then Luda would bring Mario, her special guest—it was more than a year now—his glass of Georgian tea. Sometimes he hardly heard her come in, for the thick carpeting muffled the sound of her footsteps. But when it was twenty degrees below zero and the east wind rattled his window, he would take a flask of Armenian brandy from his bottom drawer and offer her some. She didn't drink, but she accepted a cigarette. He would try out a newly learned Russian phrase. Luda would answer in a babble of Russian that Mario could barely understand. Then she would leave his room to keep guard at the landing.

For Mario, the simple hotel room had saved his sanity. He arrived between ten and eleven each night, as much to write as to escape the babies' crying, Lucia's complaints about the cold, the monotony of diplomatic dinners. He usually went home at about two in the morning. And all thanks to Michael Petrov.

Everyone suspected Michael Petrov, but Mario felt superior to the cold-war prejudices of his diplomatic colleagues. Petrov had read Dante in Italian, and Mario found him the only man in Moscow with whom he could discuss Italian literature. It was Petrov who had arranged for Mario to rent a room at the Rossiya—except for the two peak summer tourist months—to write his poetry. Last Sunday night at Rabichov's, Petrov had hinted that a special arrangement might be made for Mario to keep the room in summer as well.

Mario sipped the strong tea. He was chilly, and the tea had got cold. He poured himself a brandy. The phone rang. It had to be Lucia.

"Signor Campini," said a Russian voice in thickly accented Italian. "*Scusi.* We do not wish to trouble you, but one of your countrymen here is disturbing the hotel guests."

Mario was impatient. "Why don't you throw him out on the street?"

"It's more serious than that," the Russian voice continued. "The Italian is a guest at the hotel. He is intoxicated and has already broken furniture in his room. He is destroying Soviet property, Signor Campini. Perhaps we should call your ambassador."

"No, no. It's too late to call him. I'll come right down. What's the room number?"

"His room is on the same floor as yours. Go down the corridor and then turn right, behind the small staircase. Room 751."

Mario left his papers on the desk. Perhaps he might write more, later.

Outside Room 751, he heard low voices in Russian and opened the door.

A mass of red flowered curtains was heaped on the floor; splintered ends of broken curtain rods stuck out from under the shapeless humps. Nearby, a night table lay on its side; its single empty drawer was half open.

"You are Signor Campini?" asked a large Russian sitting back in an armchair, his white-maned leonine head secured thickly on portly shoulders. A pearly stickpin pierced his red silk tie. He made a broad gesture with his arm. "As you see, signor, it is a mess tonight."

"But where's the Italian?" Mario walked over to the pile of curtains and rods. Then he heard a click. He spun around. Behind the door, a hunchbacked young man held a camera.

"Routine. We must have a photograph of the disorder. Don't worry about it, Signor Campini," said the large Russian. He straightened an upturned chair next to him. The lapels of his gray worsted suit strained open around his wide chest. "Please sit down."

Mario was annoyed. "I don't have time, and I don't see very much damage to Soviet property except for a cheap window rod. Where's my Italian?"

"We will come to everything in good order. First, let me offer you something to drink."

"I've just had some tea, thank you."

"Ah, yes. Luda has already brought you your midnight tea."

"How do you know that?" Mario asked.

"There are few secrets from me in this hotel." He smiled broadly. His front teeth were all gold.

"Are you the manager?" Mario asked.

"In a manner of speaking, Signor Campini. But let us not talk about me."

"Let's talk about the drunken Italian," Mario persisted.

"There is no drunken Italian, Signor Campini. We simply wanted to talk to you privately."

"I am available for private discussion at my embassy, every morning at ten." He turned to leave as Luda came in. She carried a tray with two glasses of tea and two jiggers of vodka. She placed it carefully on the low table between the two chairs. Then she gave Mario a small smile and left. Mario sat down on the chair the Russian had turned upright for him.

The Russian lifted the small glass. "To Soviet-Italian friendship, Mario. You don't mind if I call you Mario? You may call me Konstantin."

Mario watched him drink. When he finished, he smacked his lips. Then he placed his hand on Mario's knee.

"You do enjoy your room here, do you not?"

"Very much. That's why I pay three hundred rubles a month."

Konstantin leaned back in his chair. "Ah, my dear Mario, having a special privilege in this country is not a matter of money."

"Come to the point, Konstantin. You want to take away my room?"

"Quite the contrary, my friend. I want you to keep it as long as you like."

"At a slight increase in rent?" Mario smiled.

"I, Konstantin, never discuss money. I find it . . . vulgar." He offered Mario a cigarette from his gold case, leaned forward, and lit it for him with an elaborate gesture of the match.

"You know, Mario, the life of a writer suits you far better than the routine of a diplomat. I know, I know, you don't have to answer. To write is a great gift, but it often goes unrecognized. We Russians love literature, especially poetry. It is absolutely essential for the soul. And you, Mario, are especially gifted. . . ."

"How would you know?" Mario interrupted. "Can you judge poetry in Italian?"

"Let us say that qualified friends have read your verse and esteem it highly. You owe it to your country, to world culture, to devote more time to your poetry."

Mario put out his cigarette. "Thank you, tovarich. I am flattered. And I would be grateful if I could keep the room during the summer months. . . ."

"I was hoping that you would say that, my friend. Because I wish to offer you an opportunity to use the room not only during winter nights, but during daytime hours as well, without any inhibitions. You could tell your ambassador, of course, that you had an official appointment outside the embassy."

Mario raised his eyebrows. "What would I tell him when I got back?"

Konstantin was pleased. "Nothing. No explanation would be necessary, that's the beauty of it. You would return with an attaché case full of information for your ambassador, highly interesting information." He winked at Mario. "That outside appointment will greatly enhance your career as a diplomat."

"And how would I earn my attaché case full of information—by writing an ode to Lenin?"

"You have a sense of humor, Mario, that's good. But I am thinking of an easier way, a more balanced arrangement. Let us call it an exchange of information."

"Sorry, Konstantin, but I'm afraid I'm not your type. Spies are born. . . ."

"Why do you call it spying?" Konstantin was annoyed. "I have said nothing about spying, have I?"

"Call it anything you want, Konstantin. I make it my business to know nothing that would be of any interest to you or any other member of the KGB."

"I, Konstantin, have absolutely nothing to do with the KGB. Quite the contrary. My interests, and those of my associates, are rather different from those of the KGB. We have asked you here tonight to help vindicate the honor of the Soviet Army. Specifically, the reputation of a great man, a great general, Pyotr Alexandrovich Zhalkov."

"General Zhalkov? I hardly even know him."

"Knew him. The general died three months ago. The Saturday before his death, his last hours in Moscow before returning to Leningrad, he spent at the dacha of your ambassador. It is imperative that we know what they discussed."

"I wasn't there. I know nothing about it."

"You enjoy the full confidence of your ambassador, Mario. He would tell you about their discussion, if you made it your business to find out."

"It is none of my business—nor yours, for that matter."

"There you are wrong, my friend. What the late General Zhalkov may have told your ambassador a few days before his death is of great concern to us all. It is the concern of everyone interested in world peace."

"You've lost me, Konstantin. A Soviet general dies. That happens almost every month, according to your own obituaries. Except this general happens to have had lunch at my ambassador's. So what?"

"Let me speak more plainly, Mario, and perhaps you will understand our position. General Zhalkov did not die naturally." The burly Russian paused to let the silence emphasize the import of his words. "He was killed."

Mario put his hands over his ears. "I don't want to hear. Don't tell me any more. This is an internal affair of the Soviet Union, and I want no part of it." He jumped up and walked quickly toward the door. "Tell me, Konstantin, do you want me out of the room tonight or do I have till the end of the month?"

Despite his weight, the portly Russian sprang up swiftly from the chair and strode toward Mario.

"You take our conversation very lightly, Signor Campini. For more than a year, you have enjoyed the privilege of a highly esteemed guest. You show no gratitude. We allow you to get drunk in your room. . . ."

"That's not true. I've never. . . ."

"Show him the photo, Fedya." The little hunchback pulled a picture out of the camera and handed it to Konstantin.

"You see how drunk you get, my friend. You even pull down curtains and push over night tables." He held out the picture at arm's length for Mario to see.

"But this was just taken when I entered the room. Tonight. Fifteen minutes ago."

Konstantin studied the picture. "Was it? I don't remember. But we have other pictures too. Would you like to sit down and we can look at them together?" Mario refused to budge. "All right, then, as a good host, I shall remain standing, too." He took a brown envelope from his breast pocket and slid out a handful of four-by-six glossies. "Ah, yes, in this one, my dear Mario, your face is very clear."

Mario pulled the photograph from Konstantin's hand. It was a picture of him making love to Claudia. Taken when? His memory raced back. Nearly two years ago. Still in Rome. A week before he had left for Moscow. Dinner on the Piazza Navona, a brandy on the Piazza del Popolo. A final good-bye for old times' sake.

"You bastards! You dirty-minded monsters!"

"I would not talk about dirty minds, Signor Campini. It is you who are doing these things. I just happen to be in possession of the photographs."

"And you think you're going to blackmail me with them. I congratulate you, Konstantin. The thoroughness of your Soviet *apparat* impresses me. You start your file on a man before he's even left for Moscow."

"Before he's left? No. I don't believe Luda was ever out of the Soviet Union."

It took Mario a minute. "Luda? That's not Luda. I've never touched Luda."

Konstantin shuffled through the old photographs. "Isn't it? It looks like her. Perhaps it might resemble another woman you know, but"—he smiled benignly— "your Foreign Office unfortunately will not be sure that it is not our own Soviet Luda."

"You're a bastard, Konstantin, but I won't play your game. My Foreign Office doesn't give a damn whom I sleep with here or in Rome." Mario turned to leave. "Keep your dirty pictures. Maybe you can get foreign currency for them."

"But Mario, *caro*, you misunderstand me. The Soviet government is also indifferent toward these pictures. But your ambassador might care very much if. . . ."

"Go tell my ambassador," Mario shouted. "He will never believe you."

Konstantin was quite calm. "I'm sure your ambassador has great confidence in you, Mario. You deserve it. Everyone will believe you. But would they trust you again, my friend? Trust you . . . completely? I would suspect that in your future career in the Foreign Office, there would always be a little shadow, a small question mark next to your name. It is only natural. You are a writer, Signor Campini. Surely you know human nature."

Mario stood very still. Konstantin put a hand on his

shoulder and led him back to the two chairs where they had been sitting. "You have not finished your vodka, Mario." Mario shook his head.

"Come now, my friend, we are not asking you to be a common spy. That is degrading work. For a cultured man like yourself, the task is far more subtle. Mario, you must learn to distinguish between the petty secrets that each country keeps to itself and the higher knowledge that must be shared for the common good."

"Why the devil did you have to bring these pictures into it if it's all so high-minded?"

"Let's not be petulant, Mario. I just happen to have these pictures with me this evening and thought you might want to see them. Here, take them if you like." He slid the envelope into Mario's jacket pocket. "There now"—Konstantin smiled—"let's forget about these pictures and get back to your ambassador and General Zhalkov."

Mario's glazed eyes stared ahead. *What is this monster talking about?* he thought. *I write poetry. I have nothing to do with murdered generals. I must get back to my room. I will take my papers and disappear from this hotel. And this golden-toothed pig with his dirty pictures will disappear from my life.*

". . . so you see, Mario, when you have helped us combat these dishonorable elements in our society, your life will continue as peacefully as before." He paused. "I shall expect you tomorrow at five."

"Yes, yes, that's what I want. To continue as before," Mario repeated.

"Needless to say, you are to tell no one of this evening. It will be our secret. You agree?"

"But I am not sure that my ambassador would tell me anything. . . ."

"We have full confidence in you, Mario. You will succeed." Konstantin got up and helped Mario to his feet. He placed an arm around his shoulder and walked him to the door. He put out his hand. Mario shook it limply.

Konstantin was happy. "Yes, I think we understand each other, don't you?" His teeth gleamed.

Mario walked slowly back to his room and unlocked it. He looked at the papers that he left on his desk: his half-finished poem, his scribbled notes, his jottings of meter. He gathered them all together and lay them tenderly in the drawer. He felt the brown envelope in his jacket that Konstantin had given him. He took it out and placed it on top of his papers. *I can't take it all home now. Tomorrow night. When I'm not so tired.*

He took his coat from the closet, stuffed the flask of cognac into his pocket, and walked down the corridor. As he laid the key on Luda's desk, she looked up at him.

"Good night, Gospodin Campini," she said, just as she did every night.

As Luda watched the steel elevator doors close behind him, she recognized the familiar figure ascending the carpeted stairway. She nodded silently. With his own key, Michael Petrov let himself into Room 751, where Konstantin was waiting.

Chapter Five

The doorbell woke Vannie Saturday morning. The sharp ringing followed her into the bathroom where she dashed to get a robe. As she ran through the living room, fumbling with its sleeves, the high piercing strains flooded the apartment.

"I'm coming, I'm coming," Vannie shouted. "Take your hand off the button."

The bell shrilled out above the front door, lashing her head with sharp, cutting waves. "Who's there?" she asked hoarsely, trying to get under the sound.

She heard breathing. No answer. The door was vibrating to the bell's rasping undertones. "Stop ringing," she screamed. Then she leaned her shoulder against the door and double-locked it.

She ran back into the living room. From the window, she saw two men cross the courtyard. The windows were still sealed for the winter. She rapped at the double window panes; they didn't hear. *I'm trapped. Nobody can hear me. That bell*—she put her hands to her ears— *that bell will drown me.*

"Nancy. My buddy Nancy," she repeated as she stumbled into the bedroom. She couldn't get a dial tone. She banged down the receiver and called again.

"It's me, Vannie. Please come. Right away. Someone's at the door and won't go away."

"I'll be right there," Nancy said.

Vannie shut the bedroom door to mute the sound, but the walls seemed to shake to the rhythm of the steady siren. *The bell will give out. It can't go on.*

She waited at the window. Nancy Colt, holding her coat tightly around her, was marching, unhurried, past the militia box. Vannie closed her eyes; the sounds started swirling into colors. Then the ringing stopped.

There was a knock. "It's me," Nancy said. Vannie unlocked the door and let her in.

"What are you so hysterical about?" Nancy asked.

"The bell. Somebody was pressing it. It wouldn't stop."

"Of course it wouldn't. It was stuck. With my fingernail, I just pulled the button out a little." After ten years in the foreign service, Nancy exuded an air of unflappable serenity.

Vannie smiled in gratitude. "I guess Moscow is giving me the jumps."

"Do you want me to stay with you, Vannie?"

"No, I feel better now. See." She stretched out her fingers. Chagrined by their trembling, she said, "Well, I'll feel better tonight at any rate. Once I get on the train for Leningrad."

"The overnight train? Tonight?" Nancy was surprised.

Vannie nodded. "We have a good friend there, a Russian. It's his birthday tomorrow."

"Vannie Tomkins, after all that's happened to you this week, you shouldn't be going to Leningrad alone. Wait till next weekend, and I'll go with you."

"Thanks, Nancy, but I promised months ago that I'd be there this weekend. Besides, he has nothing to do with politics; he's a musician."

"It's not him I'm worried about. It's you."

"Nancy, if our friend has the courage to invite me, am I supposed to tell him that I'm afraid to take a train by myself? I've already been a coward once this week."

"This is no time to travel alone, Vannie. Trust me. All sorts of things are happening in Moscow now."

"I know. That's just why I'm getting out of town."

"Your logic escapes me." Nancy paused a moment. "At least, go see Hardy Summers at the embassy before you leave. He's duty officer today. Please talk to him."

"About what?"

"About the search. About your stuck doorbell. . . ."

"I thought you said it was stuck accidentally."

"I'm not saying it wasn't. Listen. I don't care what you tell him. Just see him. Before you leave for Leningrad."

Vannie looked at her friend intently, but the poised, blond diplomat would say no more. Finally Vannie nodded. "I'll go now."

It was a twenty-minute walk from the compound to the American embassy—a solid ten-story stone structure whose two arched entrances were "protected," like all official buildings, by two armed Soviet militiamen. Vannie took the elevator up to the chancery on the ninth floor.

In the pine-paneled waiting room, a crew-cut marine guard dutifully proffered the official visitors' book for her signature. He added her time of arrival. "Mr. Summers is busy at the moment, ma'am. Won't you take a seat?"

While Vannie ensconced herself in a corner chair, the elevator gate in the outer hall rolled open, followed by the entrance of a new visitor.

"Are you finally coming for your cup of tea?" Vannie asked.

Sally Fields turned. "Oh, Vannie. Sorry. I was a bit lost in thought. Tea? That's right. We never did make it to your place yesterday, did we?"

"That's all right. I never sent you a reminder. I waited, but I wasn't really expecting you."

"Weren't you? Eric and I planned to come, you know. Was Yuri Zhalkov waiting too?"

Vannie winced. "No, he couldn't make it. Maybe another time."

"Maybe. But that I doubt."

"Why? Something's wrong, isn't it, Sally?"

"Wrong? No. Nothing at all. We just might be leaving tomorrow, that's all."

"For Leningrad?"

"For London." Sally clenched her teeth.

"Oh, but I thought. . . . What happened?"

"Nothing happened. Absolutely nothing. We've made

all our arrangements for Leningrad—train tickets, hotel reservations. Just our residence permits haven't come through."

"But you can't go to Leningrad without permission."

"We do have tourist visas. But it's beneath Eric's dignity to go without an academic OK."

"That's a pity."

"It's absurd," Sally agreed. "But it's not the last word yet."

Both young women turned as Hardy Summers, the embassy cultural attaché, emerged from the inner chancery offices, ushering out the Swiss chargé d'affaires.

"Bernard Fauvet," Vannie exclaimed, extending her hand. As usual, the Swiss diplomat brushed it with his moist mouth. "I didn't realize you work on Saturdays."

"*Jamais, ma petite.* I have only dropped by for a last chat with my *cher collègue* here." He smiled at Hardy. "Besides, my work in Moscow is finished. I'm leaving at the end of next week."

Vannie looked from Fauvet to Sally. The two invitations. Both of them leaving suddenly. "I didn't know your tour was over, Bernard," she said.

"It is rather unexpected," he admitted, "but I was offered a new and rather exciting post in Berne. I couldn't let it go by. A new ambassador will be arriving here in ten days, you know."

"I wish you the best of luck." Vannie hoped she sounded sincere.

"Don't say good-bye now. There will be a farewell party at the residence on Tuesday. Please come."

"I'll try," Vannie said, "if I'm back from Leningrad by then."

Fauvet leaned forward to kiss her cheek. "Remember," he winked, "behave yourself after I've gone."

Hardy Summers, rangy and relaxed in his weekend Levis and red-checkered shirt, flashed a boyish grin. "Now which of you charming ladies do I have the pleasure with first?" he said as he smoothed back a corn-colored cowlick from his forehead.

"We're scratching each other's eyes out for the privilege," Sally said. "If you don't mind, Vannie, I just have a simple question for Mr. Summers." Vannie nodded. Hardy led Sally to an antechamber off the waiting room.

The small window of the special conference room looked out on a spacious inner courtyard; surrounding the same courtyard were three tall Soviet buildings.

"Extraordinary," said Sally as she leaned back in the leather chair facing the window. "The Russians could so easily pick up all your conversation here at the embassy. Doesn't it give you a spooky sensation, Mr. Summers?"

"I don't think about it. Cigarette?"

"Thank you, I don't smoke. But in this room we can't be overheard. Is that correct?"

"That's what the engineers tell us."

"How divine. A truly private room. Mr. Summers, may I bring my husband here this afternoon? Would you talk to him?"

"I'm a very friendly fellow. I talk to everyone."

"I knew I could count on you. His embassy has made such a tempest in a teapot. And Eric could use a little of your personal assurance that there's no danger in our staying a little longer in Russia."

"Just a minute. This is, strictly speaking, none of my business. Your husband is a British subject, and the Brits told him to clear out and take you with him."

"They do exaggerate, don't they?" She smiled. "My gold pencil gets stolen by a couple of common hooligans, and they want to bundle us out as if we were the criminals. It's absurd, isn't it?"

Hardy Summers looked at her sharply. "Consider yourself lucky. Nastier things sometimes happen to girls who carry pencils with a hollow center."

Sally avoided his scrutiny. "You're so right, Mr. Summers. They could have taken my watch or my rings. I suppose I did get off lightly. You know, hiding the list in my pencil was really Eric's idea. The list of names was so terribly important to his thesis, he didn't want to take any chance on misplacing it." She leaned forward. "I'll tell you a secret. I've memorized the names. And as soon as Eric calms down, I think I could persuade him to go up to Leningrad and see at least a few of those people. Why do you look surprised? His embassy can't force us to leave, after all."

"Are you innocently or deliberately ignoring the fact that General Zhalkov's name was on that list?"

"Oh, dear, let's not fuss about that again. To Eric and me, General Zhalkov was simply another name, no more important than any other survivors of the Leningrad siege. But when the Brits heard that General Zhalkov was on our list, they just exploded. They wouldn't hear of our going to Leningrad or even staying on in Moscow. Don't you find the British frighten rather easily? They've so intimidated Eric he's nearly expecting the KGB to shoot him in front of the Winter Palace. Isn't it ridiculous?"

"Let's get a couple of things straight. Your talking to survivors of the Leningrad siege is inviting trouble from the KGB at any time."

"Now how would the KGB know what kind of list that was? After all, they were just ordinary hooligans who stole my gold pencil."

"Says you, they were."

"Now, Mr. Summers, you are perfectly aware of the circumstances of that theft," Sally protested. "I've already explained how I was held up in the vestibule of Sasha Rabichov's building. My money was taken, the bundles of clothing. And the pencil. I guess because it looked expensive. The hooligans themselves probably don't know there's a list of names in the hollow."

"And when they find out?" Hardy asked.

"That may not be for a long time. Maybe never. So Eric could really continue his work here. Even in Leningrad. A word from you. . . ."

"You expect me to say that it was a mere coincidence that your gold pencil with the name of General Zhalkov was stolen the day after the announcement of his assassination?"

"What else could it be?" Sally smiled sweetly.

"At the moment I don't know. I just know what you told us. More than that I don't know, do I? Maybe your husband will buy your story, maybe even the Brits. But I don't."

"Mr. Summers, are you suggesting that I'm lying?"

"No, ma'am, I'm just telling you, as nicely as I know how, that your story smells awful bad. And before it gets any worse, I think you'd better pack up and leave."

Sally rose. "Is that your official position, Mr. Summers?"

"Hell, no. It's farm-boy intuition. We smell musk a mile off. So does the KGB."

"If we're going to be primitive about this, Mr. Summers, I'd just as soon leave."

"Atta girl. You take the plane out tomorrow and don't give us any more problems." He opened the door and led her to the marine desk. "I think you'd better sign in, honey. The rules, you know."

Sally waved the visitors' book away. "Why don't you sign for me, Mr. Summers? And don't forget to write in the time of departure. Let's not skip any of the rules today." She extended her hand. "Good-bye. It's been terribly pleasant talking to you. I shall always remember the courage of my fellow Americans." Then, turning toward Vannie: "Sorry I took so long, darling. The gentleman was stubborn. I trust you'll have better luck."

Chapter Six

The Soviet Cultural Exchange had finally called Eric Fields on Friday morning, five days after Rabichov's party, asking him to report to their office at four o'clock. At last they were responding to Eric's request, submitted three weeks earlier, for permission to continue his research in Leningrad, accompanied, of course, by his wife. Eric and Sally Fields had spent the past six months preparing for the trip with single-minded tenacity.

It was no secret that Eric Fields' research project concerned the wartime siege of Leningrad. No one had objected; the subject was academically permissible. Yet when he and Sally had first started questioning students at the university or even painters they met at Rabichov's, the mere allusion to the nine-hundred-day siege evoked a shrug of the shoulder, an uncertain eye casting about for a hidden microphone.

German bombardment had killed a slender fraction of the two million dead; Leningrad had been left to starve. After the war, Moscow explained it as a military necessity. Few Russians Eric talked to believed it. Had Stalin secretly abetted the extinction of the old Leningraders, with their memories of royalty and revolution? To document his thesis, Eric would have to seek out responsible Leningrad figures who had survived both the wartime siege and the postwar purge of the city's leaders.

With their candid manner and fluent Russian, Sally and Eric Fields had extracted from friends a dozen names and addresses of prominent Leningrad survivors, including that of General Pyotr Zhalkov. Aware that their tiny furnished room in the foreign students' hostel was frequently searched by the KGB "cleaning woman," they kept the list of Leningrad names rolled tightly inside the hollow of Sally's gold pencil.

Eric wondered why the Cultural Exchange had not asked that Sally accompany him; she, too, would need a residence permit for Leningrad. But, for once, Moscow inefficiency suited him. If he were delayed at the Cultural Exchange, Sally could get to Vannie Tomkins' by five. It was important to see Yuri Zhalkov again. Was he, indeed, related to the general from Leningrad? Curious manners in Russia; he had spoken to Yuri for nearly an hour at Rabichov's on Sunday without learning his last name. It was Sally who had supplied him with it on the way home. But in the excitement of the party, she had not made the connection.

Sally was always pleased to spend an afternoon unchaperoned. Before taking tea at Vannie's, she would go to Sasha Rabichov's. He, too, had called before lunch, asking her to bring the "gift" to his studio not later than three thirty. Sasha was referring to their sheepskin coats and boots, which she had promised him at the cocktail party. Sally and Eric felt indebted to Sasha: He had introduced them to many Russians, several of whom provided their contacts in Leningrad. Sasha would undoubtedly sell the "gift" on the black market.

Sally rolled the two bundles of clothing in brown paper, securing them with knotted bits of string. Eric carried the heavier bundle as they walked toward the taxi stand. Ten yards from the dormitory, a tan Moskvich cab pulled up slowly to the curb in front of them. Eric put both bundles in the front seat next to the driver.

"If I don't get to Vannie's in time, you do remember what to ask?"

"Don't rush. I'll manage." Sally blew him a kiss and shut the taxi door. Settling back in her seat, she smiled secretly to herself: *Married nearly a year and he still thinks I can't be trusted with something important.* Sally was proud that she, not Eric, had secured most of the names in Leningrad. She could elicit information without seeming to try. It wouldn't be difficult with Yuri Zhalkov—she might even make him grateful for the privilege.

Sally Redford Fields had always managed her own life. At Blue Grass Junior College, she chose her dates from the less fashionable part of town. After refusing her coming-out cotillion, she took her allowance to London, where her demure surface was accepted as breeding, a perfect cover for random explorations. There she let Eric Fields persuade her that academia could be exciting. And she persuaded him that new experience in foreign countries was thoroughly in keeping with the highest traditions of Empire.

The sun came out as her taxi passed the Kremlin, lighting up its onion-shaped domes. The driver took an unfamiliar route through narrow cobblestone streets, passing abandoned wooden huts, relics of nineteenth-century Moscow waiting patiently to be demolished. The driver stopped at a red light. When it turned green, the taxi failed to start.

The driver got out, opened the hood and peered inside. Another tan Moskvich pulled up ten feet ahead of them. Sally thought of switching cabs, but the other was occupied. Then the other driver got out and joined hers beneath the raised hood. She couldn't see the two passengers leaving the second taxi.

She was looking at her watch, which had stopped. She started to wind it. Then suddenly, both doors opened at once. From each side a man slid in beside her, slamming the door behind him. Her driver returned to his seat. With a jolt, the taxi sped off.

Sally thought she ought to scream. But hysteria wasn't her style. Besides, who among the grubby pedestrians might possibly care what happened to her? Moscow was the city of supreme indifference. Sally would look after herself; she had learned how long before coming to Russia.

"Where are we going?" she managed to ask lightly.

"You'll see," the pudgy youth at her left answered. He looked like a farm boy, with blooming red cheeks and thick, milk-fed lips. He pressed up against her, his open raincoat spreading onto her lap, a camera clutched in his left hand. The dark man at her right, with his pinstriped suit and long sideburns, looked like a Latin dandy. He smoked a cigarette with concentrated detachment.

"Do you have the correct time?" she asked him.

He exposed a hairy wrist. She set her watch by his.

The taxi pulled up to a three-story yellow stucco house, dwarfed between new red-brick housing. She had passed the building many times without noticing it. At the end of the street, she could see the mesh fence that surrounded the foreigners' compound where the Tomkinses lived.

The dandy got out first. His round-faced lackey gathered the bundles from the front seat and followed them up the drafty wooden staircase to the top floor. There was only one door. It was unlocked.

The small, square room contained a single gray-streaked window facing the rear courtyard. A faded khaki-colored blanket lay carelessly over a lumpy mattress. In the far corner, a bridge table covered with a fresh white cloth was set for three.

The pudgy youth dropped the bundles as well as his camera in front of the window and, without taking off his raincoat, sat down to eat. Sally lay her coat on the bed and, without hesitating, took her place between the two men.

She was determined not to lose her cool. It was a party. It had begun unusually. But if she had learned anything in Moscow, it was not to question. At least not too soon. They would probably talk over coffee.

Sally helped herself to some limpid caviar, smearing it on a bit of dark bread. Then the dark-haired dandy raised his tumbler of vodka and nodded to her. Sally knew she could hold her liquor. She took her glass, and they both drank.

The pudgy youth slapped two thick slices of bread around a slab of cheese. Sally nibbled at her caviar sandwich; the vodka was strong. The dandy turned to her, smiled, and raised his glass in a silent toast. She smiled back, pleased, and drank again, emptying the glass. It wasn't so bad after all. Sally started to enjoy herself.

Then he lifted his arm and stretched it toward her. She wanted to raise her hand to shake his. But somehow she couldn't lift her hand from the table. His hand reached over her plate and pinched the nipple of her left breast.

She tried to move back her chair, but it wouldn't budge. His left hand reached over the bread and grasped her other breast. His long slim fingers squeezed and turned her protruding nipples as if finely tuning a pair of stereo knobs.

Sally sat staring ahead of her. She saw the fat youth grab a piece of honey cake. The dandy puffed on his cigarette. And then she felt the pulse beating between her legs. She couldn't move.

He got up and brought an ashtray to the table. He left his cigarette burning on the rim and bent down beside her chair. Sally's body was limp.

He lifted her skirt, pushed her thighs apart, and slipped his hand into the crotch of her panties, massaging her mound. His fingers were cold. "She's ready," he said.

She saw the fat boy put a radish in his mouth. She felt the smoke from the dandy's burning cigarette in her nostrils. (She remembered thinking: *He's not sending me to Siberia.*) Then, suddenly, she felt his sulfurous heat against her face. She remembered nothing more.

She awoke on the bed, feeling bruised. She was certain that she hadn't screamed. Were those her white panties under the lunch table? She raised herself upright but felt dizzy.

The dark man, his shirt sleeves rolled up, was drinking a cup of black coffee. The pudgy youth, still wearing his raincoat, bit ravenously into an apple. Then he spat, the apple pit jetting across the room onto the rumpled bed. "You drink too much. Doesn't she, Boris?"

"That's enough, Misha. Go downstairs now." The farm boy put a banana in his pocket, slung the camera over his shoulder, and left.

"Now that you have had your little sleep, drink some coffee." He handed her a mug as she rose weakly from the bed. She sipped it. It was sweet and tepid.

She stared at the half-eaten food and dirty plates in front of her. He watched her.

"Suppose you tell me where you were going with your bundles."

"First you tell me what happened this afternoon . . . between you and me. Or was that farmhand . . . ?"

His voice was edgy. "I'll ask the questions. You answer them."

Sally's voice was bright. "In my country, we play give-and-take."

"In our country, we don't play." He got up abruptly and walked to the window. Sally sat down at the table and turned her back to him. She heard him strike a match.

"All right, Boris. That is your name, isn't it?" He didn't answer. Sally felt more comfortable not having to look at him.

"I was bringing my bundles to a friend who wants to keep warm. A simple act of generosity."

"Generosity is never simple." He paused. "What do you owe Sasha Rabichov?"

"How well informed you are, Boris!"

"That's my business. What's yours?"

"Me? I just help my husband with his work."

"As his courier?"

"His what? I mean his work at the university."

"Soviet authorities have given your husband permission to study at our university. You spend your time collecting names and addresses. Why?"

She shrugged her shoulders. "We've made friends. You forget there is no public telephone book in Moscow. If I didn't write them down, how would I remember their numbers?"

"Not Moscow. Leningrad. These addresses." She turned around. He held her gold pencil and pulled out the tip. She saw the slip of paper that she had tucked into the hollow.

"Oh, that. It's a special list in connection with my husband's thesis. I didn't want to lose it."

"Who gave you the name of General Zhalkov?"

"I don't remember. Many people have been helpful."

"Including his nephew."

"I don't know his nephew. I never even met...."

"Is this your card?" From his trouser pocket he withdrew the white visiting card: "Sally Fields. Hotel Sovietskaya. April."

"You gave it to Yuri Zhalkov on Sunday. Is that where he is to contact you in Leningrad?"

"Contact? I hardly know him."

"In twenty minutes, you are due to meet him for the third time. At the house of an American correspondent. Why?"

"To talk. Chit-chat." Her voice was edgy now. The dandy knew much too much.

"What did he tell you at your first meeting? At the university. About the death of his uncle?"

"I didn't know then that General Zhalkov was his uncle. And I didn't know until this very minute he was dead."

"The news was on your BBC yesterday."

"It's not *my* BBC," she flared. "I don't even own a radio." She turned away to compose herself. Then, in soft tones, she continued, "Boris, I don't know what you're making such a fuss about. Yuri Zhalkov is from Leningrad. We want to visit Leningrad. We have asked a lot of people for names because we're interested in seeing a little more than the ordinary tourist spots. What's so unusual about that? If you were going to London tomorrow, I might give you some names and addresses. That is, if you were a little pleasanter."

There was a silence. Then he asked her, "Would you like some more vodka?"

"Not unless you're drinking from the same glass."

She heard him cross to the table and watched his hands pour the vodka from the carafe into his glass. He handed it to her.

She looked at him a moment and then backed up in her chair. "I've changed my mind. I still have a headache from the first glass."

He smiled and downed it in one swallow. "You have no courage. Only a sharp tongue."

Sally suddenly felt very weary. Her bones ached. She closed her eyes. "I'd like to go home."

"The door is open. You are free to leave." Then he added, "No one forced you. You came with us willingly. Perhaps you thought I, too, would give you an address in Leningrad?" His tone mocked her.

She rose, standing motionless as if trying to remember something.

"Your coat is on the bed. A little rumpled," he said. "Or do you want to stay?"

She picked up her coat and slipped it on.

"Don't forget your gift for Rabichov," he said.

The two bundles were on the floor in front of the window. She tried to pick them up. The string cut her fingers. She bent over and started to drag them across the floor. He watched her huddled over, amused.

Sally let them go and straightened herself upright. "No, I don't want them anymore. You keep them. The coats and the boots. I hope you swelter to death in them."

She marched across the room and slammed the door behind her.

Chapter Seven

"Hardy, tell me, does Eric Fields work for MI-5?" Vannie asked as the embassy elevator signaled Sally's descent to street level.

Hardy spun around. "Who the hell ever said that?"

"Just a rumor," Vannie replied, trying to seem nonchalant. "In this town, you never know."

"That's for sure. Best policy around here is to mind your own business and keep your nose clean." The lean attaché ambled over to the marine guard's desk.

"Then why does Sally have to leave so suddenly?"

"Search me." Hardy shrugged as he printed Sally Fields' name in the visitors' book.

"But she seemed so disturbed," Vannie persisted. "Is she or her husband in any trouble?"

He glanced up at the clock before adding Sally's time of departure. "As far as I'm concerned, it's a personal matter between the two of them."

Vannie rose and placed her hand on Hardy's arm. "I'm not asking out of pure curiosity," she said gravely. "I think I ought to know."

"Shall we move in there?" He gestured amicably toward the antechamber.

She shook her head. "I'd rather not. I don't like to talk in rooms, even your special, bug-proof one. Why don't you take me for a walk instead? It's spring outside."

"Good idea. Let me get my coat."

Upon leaving the embassy, they received a cheerful salute from the burly militiaman standing beside the sentry box. His colleague, inside the wooden booth, jotted down their names and picked up the telephone to report.

Vannie and Hardy Summers walked with their coats unbuttoned in the unusual mildness of the April day. They turned away from the new Kalinin Prospekt—the latest Potemkin Village of soaring glass and aluminum—and headed toward the broad stone bridge spanning the Moskva. The multi-towered and -turreted Hotel Ukraina squatted over the river's south bank like an ocher-colored wedding cake.

Vannie followed Hardy through a recessed archway connecting twin red-brick apartment houses to reach a flagstone path overlooking the river embankment. Families from the neighborhood were strolling under the midday sun. But they kept their overcoats buttoned and their children bundled in boots and mufflers. The patches of old winter snow, speckled with black city soot, would have to melt and dry before Muscovites believed in spring.

"Well," Vannie began, "now that we're far away from everybody's bugs, can you tell me why Fauvet is leaving Moscow?"

"He told you, didn't he?"

"Now really, Hardy! No job in Berne could tear him away from his stuffed grouse. Have the Russians forced Bernard to leave? Or is that, too, something between him and his wife?" Vannie asked archly.

"Vannie, you know a lot more than you think you do. Why are you asking me questions like Alice in Wonderland?"

"All right. Keep the great big diplomatic secret to yourself. But can you at least tell me if his leaving has anything to do with me?"

"That's for you to say, Vannie."

"Look, Hardy, I didn't come to the embassy to pour out my life story. It was Nancy who thought I ought to check with you."

"What about?" Hardy smiled.

"My doorbell. It was ringing this morning for a quarter of an hour. I was scared. But you don't think the KGB is after me?"

"Just because your doorbell was ringing."

She hesitated a moment. "No. I also know General Zhalkov's nephew."

"How well?"

"What is that supposed to mean?"

"Just a routine question. But if you've been in any situation with a Russian that you might be ashamed of. . . ."

"It's very tactful of you to limit any possible *flagrante delicti* to situations with Russians. The answer is, No, Mr. Summers, I've been such a good girl I could scream."

"Then don't scream too loud and you'll have nothing to worry about. . . . Unless, of course," he added slowly, "there's something else. . . ."

Vannie glanced at him sideways. "You're playing cat and mouse with me. Nancy told you, didn't she? About the KGB search at my friends'?" Hardy nodded.

"Just as well, I suppose," Vannie continued. "But I didn't tell her . . . I think . . . Fauvet may be leaving because of me. I did something stupid."

"Don't look now, Vannie. Just sort of turn slightly to your left. The river's pretty, isn't it? Now tell me if that man in the brown suit is a friend of yours."

Vannie turned, too quickly perhaps. "You mean that one drinking from the vodka bottle? The drunk? I've never seen him before in my life."

Hardy smiled. "Lovely day. Come, let's get an Eskimo pie. The ice cream stand is just between those buildings there. Turn around, naturally now, like we haven't noticed anybody. OK."

Hardy treated. He took a cone and handed Vannie a chocolate sandwich. "The best consumer product in the Soviet Union," he announced.

Vannie was about to agree. "My God, Hardy, there he is again. The one in the brown suit. He's bending over to tie his shoelace, right in front of us."

"Don't make such a fuss, old girl. This is probably his beat. Just look the other way." Hardy licked the ice cream off his fingers. "You started to tell me about Fauvet."

Vannie cast another quick glance at the "drunk" in

the brown suit. The ice cream was melting in her hand. "I don't want this anymore."

"Give it to me. I'll finish it. Now what exactly happened between you and Fauvet?"

"Happened? With him? God, no, I'm not that desperate. But he sent me an invitation for the general's nephew. The KGB found it in my bag. They made a big fuss about it, as if I were running a messenger service between him and Fauvet."

"How well did Fauvet know Yuri Zhalkov?"

"How do *you* know his name?"

"Nancy mentioned it."

"She couldn't have. I've never told Nancy the names of any of my Russian friends."

Hardy shrugged his shoulders. "These things get around."

Vannie raised her eyebrows. "So do you, apparently," she said. Hardy was silent.

"Come, Vannie, let's walk this way." He steered her arm.

"Why?" Vannie looked around. "I don't see the man in the brown suit. Just those . . . Hardy, they're only college kids!"

"Old enough to earn a living. Let's walk naturally, shall we? There's an empty bench over there." He pressed her arm. "Vannie, stop staring at them!"

The bench overlooked the river. Vannie lit a cigarette.

"I thought you kicked the habit."

"I started again last Monday. When I came home after the search, I smoked up a chimney."

"Nancy said the search took place on Wednesday," Hardy said.

"No. I told her about it Wednesday evening."

"It was on Monday then," Hardy repeated slowly.

"I told them the truth—that I had never met the general, that I was coming to pose for my friend Lydia, and that Fauvet asked me to pass on a dinner invitation to Yuri."

"Whom you've known how long?"

"Oh, a couple of months."

"Exactly when did you meet him? Do you remember?"

"Some time in January. Wait a second, it was the same day as the Australian National Day reception. I had to get my hair done, so I came to Lydia's earlier than usual. Let me check."

Vannie pulled out a small red leather notebook from her handbag. She called it "My Russian Life"; it contained a record of her social engagements and the names and addresses of all her Russian friends. She always kept the book with her.

"Here it is. The twenty-seventh of January. Yuri had come down from Leningrad—I guess—about two weeks before."

"Which would be roughly three weeks after his uncle was killed." Abruptly, Hardy rose. He stretched his arm lazily. "Let's walk down by the river, Vannie."

Only then did Vannie notice the old Russian woman sitting beside her. She had quietly taken a place on the edge of the bench while Vannie's back was turned. Vannie quickly put the red address book back in her bag.

There was a steep dirt incline of about a hundred feet down to the concrete embankment. Hardy went first, taking Vannie's hand. At the bottom she was breathless.

"Not a *babushka*, Hardy! That was a harmless old lady!"

Hardy shrugged his shoulders. "I didn't say anything, did I?"

"No. As a matter of fact, you haven't said a thing. I'm doing all the talking. Can you at least tell me how you know they're following us? Actually, they're not even *following*. We seem to be walking through a grid or something. They come at us from all sides. How do you tell them from the others?"

"It's easy, friend. Real people look at foreigners—our haircuts, our shoes, coats. But 'them,' they look up at the sky, or stare straight ahead, or read newspapers—anything to avoid looking straight at you and me."

"Well, they've never stalked me like this before. Taking a casual Saturday stroll with a diplomat—wow!"

"But this isn't a casual stroll. Is it, Vannie?"

"You've been pretty casual. Until we got to Zhalkov."

"Until *you* got to Zhalkov."

"I just told you that I was asked if I knew him."

"They asked you that on Monday, Vannie," he said evenly.

"Which means what?"

"Which means the KGB thought that you, Vannie Tomkins, might know something about a murdered man three days before the news became public. It was a well-kept secret until the VOA broadcast Thursday morning.

Except perhaps to Yuri Zhalkov, whom you have been seeing since he came down from Leningrad three weeks after the assassination." He paused. "Now who should be asked whom the questions?"

"Yuri never told me anything about his uncle. I never even knew he had one until Fauvet mentioned it at a party last Sunday. And I don't know why you assume that I'm mixed up in the Zhalkov affair."

"Vannie, I'm not assuming anything. I'm telling you that the KGB may suspect you're more involved than you actually are."

"Do you think the KGB also suspect the Fieldses?" Vannie asked quietly.

"The KGB suspect their own grandmothers."

"Damn it, Hardy, help me out. Just a little. Are the Fieldses mixed up with the Zhalkov case or not? Is that why they're leaving so suddenly?"

"Why is that so important for you to know?"

"Because I had two invitations in my bag during the search at my friend's. One was Fauvet's invitation. The other was my letter to Eric and Sally asking them to tea with Yuri."

"For what day?"

"Friday. Yesterday. At five. Nobody showed up."

"Then you haven't seen Zhalkov since the search?"

"Yuri? No. I suppose I should, shouldn't I?"

"No," Hardy replied flatly. "Leave well enough alone. He's got enough troubles."

"You don't think they suspect *him* of his uncle's murder? If you'd only met him, Hardy, you'd know that he couldn't be involved in anything like that."

"What does 'involved' mean? He's his nephew, isn't he? And he left Leningrad three weeks after his uncle died, however he died. Just that alone—by definition—means he's involved. Keep away, will you?"

"The VOA said that Zhalkov might have been assassinated by an officer," Vannie said quietly. "You don't agree?"

"I have no opinion. That's internal politics. Not my beat."

"If it's so internal, why did a pigeon have to take the story out of the country for anybody even to learn that General Zhalkov was dead?"

"You've done some intelligence work, I see."

"And Fauvet leaving suddenly—and the Fieldses leaving suddenly—and Campini from the Italian embassy—you think none of them has anything to do with the Zhalkov case?"

"You may know more about it than I do, Vannie. As far as I'm concerned, it's pure coincidence until proved otherwise. Lots of people leave in the spring."

Vannie was about to protest, then fell silent. She had no proof. Eric Fields might or might not work for MI-5, but she was certain that he had never met General Zhalkov; it was she, Vannie, who had introduced Eric to Yuri. Sally had said that she met Yuri at a students' party, but she hadn't even known his name was Zhalkov. Fauvet had met Yuri for the first time at Rabichov's. Had he known

101

the general? She couldn't member—all Bernard had said was that Zhalkov had been a friend of his former ambassador. Mario Campini knew neither the general nor Yuri; it was Federico Succioli who had met the general in Rome.

What was the connection? Were there any connections at all? Or was it just KGB "spring cleaning," as Federico had called it? Vannie realized how little she actually knew, and even that little had been learned by chance. Had she not expectedly dropped by the embassy this morning, she wouldn't have learned that the Fieldses and Fauvet were leaving on short notice. Federico had told her about Mario only because she had come early and pressed him, when he was still under a strain. Nancy had done nothing but caution her to stay home. And Hardy had explained nothing. The whole damned city seemed to be locked in a conspiracy of silence.

"And my ringing doorbell this morning, Hardy? Was that coincidence, too?"

"Vannie, you can't be seriously asking me if your stuck doorbell is connected to the death of a general in Leningrad."

"I'm not talking about just any stuck doorbell," Vannie flared. "I'm asking if you think the KGB is trying to put pressure on me."

"Maybe. But then I'd think they'd try something more forceful than a stuck doorbell. Don't you?"

"Such as?"

"Any number of things. Travel restrictions. They

could refuse you permission to go outside the twenty-five-mile limit around Moscow, for example."

"But they haven't. I'm leaving for Leningrad tonight."

"From the frying pan into the fire," he mused. "Whom are you going with?"

"Myself."

"Why don't you wait until Ken comes back? Where is he now, by the way—London?"

"Now don't you start that. I told Nancy he'll be in Rome until next week. And I'm expected at a birthday party in Leningrad tomorrow night. It won't wait."

Hardy thought for a minute. "Call me later this afternoon. I'll ask around. Maybe somebody from the embassy is going up to Leningrad tonight."

"What do you expect me to do—take a bodyguard along? Good Lord, I'd have half the KGB watching every move I make. Like this afternoon. I'll just go my own quiet way, thank you. I also have my Russian friends to protect, you know."

"And who protects you, Vannie?"

"I don't need it. It's my Russians who take the risks. I can just see my friend's face if I arrived at his birthday party with a 'buddy.' I'd be ashamed of myself." Vannie paused for breath. "You know, Hardy, if we Americans don't show a bit of courage in this country, why should we expect the Russians to?"

"Have it your way, Vannie. I was just trying to help."

The Hotel Ukraina loomed up at the end of the river

embankment. "Hardy, if you really want to help, there is something. I bought two paintings here—abstracts. Would you send them out for me in the diplomatic pouch?"

"I'm sorry, Vannie, I can't. It's against government regulations."

"Well, that's that, isn't it? When the squeeze is on, everybody has to fend for himself."

"Vannie, if you like, leave the paintings with me. When I'm reposted next year, I'll try shipping them out with my own stuff."

"Thank you, Hardy, but I don't want to complicate your life."

They walked silently to the end of the embankment. A dirt path led them to the rear gardens of the Ukraina. Hardy steered her through an arched passageway that opened onto a rectangular interior courtyard. Two wiry young men in baggy raincoats were slouched against the hotel façade, staring down at their feet. Vannie turned around. Hidden in the shadow of the passageway from which they had just emerged, a dark-skinned Tatar puffed intently on a long-filtered *papirosa*.

Vannie grabbed Hardy's arm. "Who are these people?"

"Calm down, girl. They're just the unemployed proletariat."

She grasped his arm still tighter. "But we're in a dead end!"

"Around the hedge, there's a path that leads straight

to Kutuzovsky Prospekt. At that point, you'll be exactly three blocks from home."

Vannie released her grip. "Well, that's just where I'm going now. I'll leave you to your KGB rat pack. Unless," she added mockingly, "you want me to walk you back to the embassy for protection."

Hardy laughed. "I think I'll manage myself. I'm a big boy, you know."

"And I'm a big girl—old enough to get a few straight answers."

"What makes you think I have them, Vannie?"

"Because it's your goddamn business."

"Take it easy, kiddo."

"How can I take it easy when you won't give me a single clue to what's going on?"

Hardy said nothing.

"All right, keep your diplomatic secrets. I'm getting out of town. I'll send you a picture postcard from Leningrad."

"It's your decision, old girl. Just remember"—he placed a hand on her shoulder—"be good."

She shook it off. "Who, me? No danger, Hardy. I never talk to strangers. Only to known agents of the KGB or CIA." Vannie curtsied to him, unsmiling, and walked briskly away.

Chapter Eight

The Krasnaya Strela—the Red Arrow—leaves Moscow at 11:53 every night, and at 11:51 Vannie was still running along the platform of the Leningrad Station. Ivan Fyodorovich, the driver, sprinted ten paces behind her, huffing and puffing with her one small suitcase in his hand. The first-class compartments were at the far end of the platform.

The engine started churning. Vannie ran faster. The driver had slowed down to a comfortable trot. *"Bistro, bistro,"* Vannie shouted breathlessly over her shoulder.

Damn Ivan, Vannie thought, *if I miss this train, it's his fault.* Five shortcuts to the Leningrad Station, but none of them good enough for him. He insisted on taking the main boulevards, pausing at every single red light, absolutely certain that all Moscow stared with envy when he, Ivan Fyodorovich, drove his big *Amerikanskaya machina.*

The Krasnaya Strela started to inch forward.

"Wait, wait," Vannie cried. *"U menya yest billet, pervi klass."* The conductor took a step down and extended his arm. Vannie grabbed it and climbed aboard. Ivan had barely a second to hoist the suitcase onto the train as the Krasnaya Strela pulled out of the station.

Vannie leaned against the train door, her eyes closed. Her knees were trembling, and she was breathing in short, deep gasps. "I would have died if I hadn't made it," she said aloud.

She opened her eyes in the quiet lighting of the corridor. The woman porter had already started serving tall glasses of strong Georgian tea in the compartments. "But I did make it. And I'll spend the night in style."

Now, where had she put her ticket? Ken's secretary had asked her Thursday morning if she already had her ticket to Leningrad. "No, I thought this time I might get it at the station Saturday night." Alla was aghast. "Where do you think you are, Vannie? You can't buy a berth on a sleeper at the station. Not in this country. Give me your passport and let me see what I can do."

Getting through red tape was Alla's specialty. Minutes before Vannie had to leave, Alla arrived triumphantly with the precious envelope. Without opening it, Vannie had quickly stuffed it in her bag—no, she remembered, in her coat pocket. She handed it to the conductor. He opened the envelope and looked at the complicated series of tickets.

"Madame, I'm afraid this is for a second-class compartment."

"Oh, no. My husband's secretary bought me a ticket for first class."

"See yourself. *Tvyordi klass*—hard class—one bed."

Vannie looked at him blankly, not knowing whether to argue or cry. She had once taken a second-class—or, as the Russians call it, hard-class—sleeper. She had spent a sleepless night with a snoring wife, a vodka-drinking husband, and a pretzel-munching child. It was very "interesting"—the foreigners' favorite word for unpleasant Russian experiences. Tonight Vannie was in no mood for "interesting" experiences. She wanted her first-class compartment with its soft mattress and clean sheets. She wanted the red velvet curtains and the *belle époque* lamps. She wanted her night in luxury, in limbo, away from the shabbiness and chicanery of Moscow.

"Please, I have some rubles with me. I'll pay you the difference. But let me stay in first class."

"We don't sell tickets on the train. I can't accept your money."

"Please, I'm not feeling very well. Surely there must be one compartment free. Please."

"Here, hold your ticket. I'll go into the other carriage. Perhaps there is something there."

Why hadn't Alla said she could only get a second-class sleeper? Why had she handed her the envelope without a word? Vannie closed her eyes again; *please, please God, let there be something free in first class.*

The conductor returned smiling: "There is an upper berth in the section that goes on to Helsinki."

"Oh, I'm so glad. Thank you. But how do I pay you? I do have dollars with me."

"I cannot accept money. No, I cannot accept your second-class ticket either. Here, let me take your suitcase."

Gratefully, she followed him down to the last compartment in the end train. He pulled the door open. Vannie saw a man's coat lying across the lower berth.

"You . . . you don't have a whole compartment free?"

The conductor looked shocked. "But you have the upper berth."

"I know, but perhaps you have a compartment with just a woman in it."

"There is only one woman on the train, and she is traveling with her husband. If you don't want the berth. . . ."

Vannie realized that her objection to a mixed compartment was coldly regarded as "bourgeois" prissiness. "No, no, no," she said. "It's fine. I just thought . . . no, no really. It's very nice. I'm happy to be here. Thank you."

She extended her hand, with two five-ruble notes in her palm. He pulled his hand back. "That is not necessary. Remember to be ready to get off at seven-thirty when the train arrives in Leningrad. There is no announcement in the Helsinki section."

"Thank you. Good night."

Vannie looked at the coat on the lower berth. It was a smooth navy-blue chesterfield with a dark fur collar. She started to giggle: *Well, Vannie Tomkins, you're certainly not traveling with the masses tonight.* She stood in the middle of the compartment for a moment. Then the door opened behind her.

"I'm sorry, they just gave me the upper berth. I hope you don't mind."

"Not at all. But would you prefer the lower?"

"No, no, it's fine. Really. I'm just sorry I'm. ..."

He was tall and not quite handsome. His English was perfect, but there was something—not quite an accent, perhaps an inflection—in his low voice. "There's nothing to be sorry about. There are no private compartments in Russia. Here, let me take your coat. My name is Alexander Starr."

"I'm Vannie Tomkins. I'm sorry, I'm really a bit embarrassed by this."

Alexander Starr hung her coat behind the door and turned to examine her face. He was not sure if she was genuinely embarrassed or, like many American women, faking modesty. "Would you like me to ask the conductor to find me another berth? Perhaps there is a single man. ..."

"This is the last berth left. That's why they gave it to me. Besides, I'm the intruder."

He smiled. "Well, then, may I offer my intruder a glass of tea? The porter has already been here, but I think the samovar is still boiling."

He closed the compartment door softly, while Vannie sank into the red velour chair by the window. The Krasnaya Strela rode along a straight line—the penciled line that Czar Nicholas I had drawn with a ruler when asked where the tracks should be laid. The train cut through no cities. As Vannie watched through the frosty window, not even a village flashed by. Occasionally, the inky shadow of a remote house or a cluster of pine trees blurred the pale snow stretching endlessly northward.

The train raced the night through nowhere. Vannie unhooked the sashes, letting the velvet curtains fall together.

Alexander Starr returned with two glasses of tea and put them on the mahogany table between Vannie and the lower berth. He sat opposite her, opened the black attaché case beside him, and took out a flask of Remy Martin, VSOP. "I assume that you do not take cognac with your tea."

"Not usually. But I think tonight I need it. In the tea, please."

Vannie lifted the steaming glass with its carved metal handle and sipped the strong, fragrant tea. She closed her eyes for a moment and felt the knot in her stomach ease. She held the glass to her mouth, and as the vapor warmed her face, she suddenly felt her eyes fill and tears roll down her cheeks. Alexander Starr watched her, no longer amused. He handed her his handkerchief. As Vannie accepted it, her shoulders started to shake and she burst into uncontrollable sobs. They lasted only a minute. Then she dried her eyes and smiled at him.

"I'm sorry. All I seem to be saying to you this evening is I'm sorry. But I've had a difficult few days. And somehow you giving me your handkerchief . . . I'm all right now."

He got up. "Here, why don't you stretch out? You'll relax better with your legs up." He took his coat off the bed and hung it up on top of hers behind the door. He helped her up from the chair as if she couldn't manage for herself and propped two small pillows behind her on the lower berth. He sat opposite her in the armchair and poured a small brandy into his empty glass.

"Yes. Please. Me, too. I suddenly feel cold." She swallowed it neat and felt her assurance coming back. She looked at her traveling companion. "You probably feel stuck with a hysterical woman in your compartment. But Moscow life does that to you sometimes. You don't live here, do you?"

"No. I live in London."

"But you're not English."

"No, I'm American."

"But you weren't born in America, were you?"

He smiled. "No, I was born in Riga. I came to America as a child. Any more questions?" He wasn't angry, but Vannie was embarrassed again. Everything was wrong tonight. The wrong ticket, the wrong compartment, the idiotic tears, and now her stupid questioning. And he was being so terribly nice.

"I didn't mean to interrogate you. It's just that so much has happened this week that I don't understand. So many answers I don't know."

He poured them both another brandy. "In this part of the world, Mrs. Tomkins, the answers are not so important. One must first learn the right questions."

"Please call me Vannie. But that's just it—I don't know the right questions either. Or maybe I don't ask the right people. I've been leading a perfectly normal life in Moscow for nearly two years. And then, all of a sudden, my friends are no longer my friends. My Western friends tell me to avoid my Russian friends. But those

113

same people who give me advice won't tell me the whole truth—they give me bits and snatches. I'm not saying they're lying—but they always seem to be leaving out something. Something I should know. I can't figure out the simplest things anymore. Did our driver try to get me to miss this train or not? Maybe my husband's secretary got me a second-class ticket on purpose. I don't trust anyone. Not even myself."

He offered her a cigarette and then lit it for her.

"I'm not keeping you up, am I?" Vannie asked. "Maybe you want to go to sleep."

"No, I sleep very badly on trains."

"Actually, I'm not telling you the truth either—not the whole truth. I'm starting to do the same thing that everyone else does to me."

"You don't have to tell me anything, Vannie."

"But I must tell someone," she pleaded. "Otherwise I'll go out of my mind. You see, I walked in on a KGB search a few days ago. Some really close Russian friends. Now an American diplomat tells me that one of my friends may be implicated in a murder. I don't think so, really. But I'm not sure of anything anymore. I'm afraid to go back to see them. And I'm ashamed of myself for being afraid."

"It takes a good deal of courage to trust someone in the Soviet Union." He smiled.

"But my Russian friends trust me. They have more to risk than I do. You have to trust someone—if not Russians, then your own fellow Americans. A good friend of mine, for example, is leaving tomorrow, suddenly. She says it's something to do with her visa. Well, how do I know if she's told me the truth? Maybe her husband is a spy. Even my husband. He told me he was going to Rome to talk to his foreign editor. But there are people in Moscow who suspect he went out for all kinds of other reasons. Maybe he's not even in Rome. How should I know whom to believe? It's as if everyone has suddenly abandoned me."

"You're an American, Vannie. You've probably grown up in a nice small town. . . ."

"Not so nice, Binghamton."

"You grew up among your family and friends where everyone trusts, where most people try to be honest. Suddenly you arrive in Byzantium. Moscow is not Europe, you know. Leningrad, perhaps. But Moscow was always a city of deception. Even before the Communists. How could you, with your American nature, ever hope to understand it?"

"I thought I did once. At least I trusted my friends. Not anymore."

"But you do. Or else you wouldn't be telling me all this tonight. After all, I'm a stranger on a train."

Vannie laughed. "You gave me your handkerchief. And your cigarettes. And your very good cognac. May I have just a little more?"

"All right, just a little more. But I think you need a night's sleep. Finish it up while I turn down the upper berth. Would you like to change here or down the hall?"

"I . . . I'm afraid . . . Well, I thought I would be alone

in the compartment. I didn't bring anything to change into."

He laughed. "Your trusting nature again?" He took out a pair of pajamas and a robe from his suitcase and opened the compartment door. "I give you five minutes to protect yourself from me. Are you sure you don't want the lower?"

"No, really. I'll probably be fast asleep by the time you're back." Vannie locked the door behind him, and quickly slipped off her dress, shoes and stockings. *If I'm going to sleep in my underwear, it will all smell by to-morrow. I'll sleep in my slip. It's perfectly decent.* She stepped out of her panties, rinsed them in the small basin, and hung them on the towel hook. Then she un-hooked her brassiere and laid it flat at the bottom of her berth. She climbed up and slipped between the starched sheets. *I've forgotten to unlock the door.* She climbed down, pulled back the bar, and climbed up again. *Shall I turn off the light? No, maybe he reads in bed. I should be reading in bed. I don't really feel like it. I don't feel like doing anything. Except being in limbo. Out, out, out of Moscow.* She cupped her breasts with her palms and then pressed her hands along the side of her ribs down to her hips. *How nice to have a body; I'm so tired of thinking.*

He opened the door and closed it quietly. Without looking at the upper berth, he took off his robe and sat down on his bed. "Would you like a cigarette, Vannie?"

She didn't answer.

116

"Come, come, don't play the little girl. If you would like a cigarette, just say so."

"Yes, yes, I would. Thank you." He lifted his arm without turning and held the pack of cigarettes up to her. Without getting up, she lifted one from the pack. He stood up and faced the upper berth. She sat up and leaned forward for the light. He slipped a finger under her slip strap. She shivered.

"So you found something to wear?" He looked at the sheets tucked under her arms. "You needn't protect yourself so. I shan't rape you."

"No, I'm just a little chilly."

"Would you like my coat?"

"All right. If you don't mind."

He laid his coat over her legs. Then he lay down on his bed and turned off his night-light.

"You really shouldn't smoke in bed with the light off, Mr. Starr."

"Don't you find it rather indecent to share a compartment with me and still call me Mr. Starr?"

"I'm sorry, I'm just a little nervous."

"What about?"

She laughed. "Well, I probably have to go to the ladies' room."

"You mean the toilet. Then go now, before you disturb my sleep later on."

She put out her cigarette and pulled off the sheet, making sure to keep his coat unrumpled. She placed a foot on the ladder, turned, and slowly in the dark lowered one leg and then the other. Then she felt his warm hand on the back of her calf. He didn't grab it; he just stroked it up and down. She took another step down slowly. His warm, strong hand rubbed the back of her thigh and then along the soft inside flesh. She closed her eyes and leaned her head along the rim of her upper berth, still holding onto the side of the ladder.

"Come down, Vannie. You can't stand on the ladder all night."

She stood barefoot on the floor, and his hand reached and took hers.

"Come lie beside me. I won't hurt you."

She sat down on his bed and then stretched out beside him. He didn't kiss her; he just held her and with one hand stroked her hair back from her brow. And then she put her arms around him. "Yes, please. Like this. Oh, yes, please. . . . All night."

Chapter Nine

Leningrad's colors at dawn were Venice, its cold light Amsterdam. The mint-green Winter Palace glistened in the pale northern stillness. Ice floes smacked mutely against the sides of the lone barge weaving its way slowly up the Neva. Across the river, a lilac fog hovered over the marsh islands, obscuring the slender spire of Peter and Paul Fortress. Vannie's taxi, pausing a few minutes under the windows of the Hermitage, drove on.

In the raw chill of Sunday morning, early risers walked briskly under the colonnades of the Nevsky Prospekt. Through the arches Vannie glimpsed a courtly face, a St. Petersburg face that had survived beyond its time; how remote seemed the flat masks of Moscow.

Vannie had felt somewhat foolish asking the taxi driver to take this little tour before checking into the hotel. But she wished to remain a little longer in her private limbo. She was not quite ready to forfeit her freedom to the clerks of registration and passport control.

It was as though someone else had ridden on the Krasnaya Strela. Her own wantonness shocked her. Yet she smiled as images of the night tumbled in front of the pastel-colored palaces of St. Petersburg. Yes, she should

regret it more, and she would. But not now. In a few
hours, he would be in Helsinki. She wondered if Alexander Starr was his real name.

The taxi turned past St. Isaac Square and parked in
front of the Hotel Astoria. She let the porter take her one
small suitcase—it wouldn't be *kulturny* to carry it herself. Although Alla had reserved a single room, Vannie
was accorded a suite, a large living room separated from
a bedroom alcove by thick red-velvet curtains. She
thought of ordering up breakfast, but even in the legen-
dary Hotel Astoria, where old-world memories still per-
vaded the rococo suites, room service was Soviet style; it
would take an hour and arrive cold. The restaurant off
the main-floor lobby was elegant and empty. Still feeling
giddy, Vannie ordered a breakfast of caviar and vodka.

An hour later, her head spinning slightly, she climbed
the two flights of stairs to her suite. She pulled the heavy
curtains together, enclosing herself in the darkness of the
bedroom alcove. She was all alone in a strange city. Not
even her friends knew she had arrived. No one would
telephone. No one would knock on her door. She pulled
the blanket around her shoulders and, finding her ano-
nymity delicious, slept deeply.

She awoke at five o'clock and drew a bath. Lingering
in the steaming water, she looked down at her breasts.
Just a bare trace of pleasure; it would disappear by tomorrow. "Vanessa Tomkins," she asked aloud, "have you
no remorse?" Yanking out the drain, she jumped out of
the tub. The full-length mirror on the bathroom door
caught her boyishly lean figure. "I haven't changed, I'm

still the same." Catching the pink trace on her breast, she turned away quickly. "Besides, last night was nowhere. It doesn't count." She kneeled beside the tub and, as the bathwater emptied, scrubbed away the ring of soot clinging to the rim.

She dressed slowly, pushing her boots under the bed and slipping on spring shoes. Then, in the organized fashion that Ken had taught her, she collected her things on the dressing table. The tape recorder—she would tape a cassette of Andrey's songs tonight and take it back with her to Moscow. Her birthday presents for Andrey. Makeup. Cigarettes. Her wallet. Her address—where was it? She always kept the little red leather book with her. She turned her purse upside down on the bed; scraps of paper and crumbs of tobacco wafted down on the blanket.

She ran to the closet. *In my coat, probably . . . with my ticket, like last night.* No, only her return ticket was in her pocket. She opened her suitcase, and her hands dove in, fingering each piece of clothing before throwing it over the side.

How in God's name did I forget it? It was on the dining-room table in Moscow with my passport. I must have taken it with me. The train? No, I didn't leave it on the train. He even helped me gather my things together.

She sat on the bed and covered her face with her hands: *Shame on you, Vannie Tomkins. You have lost your Russian address book. You have betrayed your friends. You silly, stupid American girl. You think you misbehaved last night; you and your Binghamton moral-*

ity. This *is immoral: to lose the book with the address of every Russian friend you have.* Her breathing caught painfully in her chest. *But Vera's number—at least I remember her phone number.* Vannie and Ken had always called Vera Ivanova upon arriving in Leningrad; she invariably met them at the hotel and guided them out to Andrey's.

Vannie left the hotel and walked casually toward the Neva, a city map and a guidebook clutched in her hand. She hoped to be taken for an ordinary tourist, discouraging the beady-eyed loiterers who permanently slouched in the lobbies or anchored themselves just outside Soviet hotels.

The golden spire of the Admiralty pierced the dusky waves of the late afternoon sun as Vannie crossed the Palace Square to join a group of German-speaking tourists surrounding the Alexander Column. When she felt certain she wasn't being followed, she slipped away and headed toward the Moika Canal.

The stately St. Petersburg town houses along the canal's gray stone embankment were now mainly ministries and museums. No more gilded droshkies pulling up to the granite façades; Anna Karenina didn't live here anymore.

Vannie crossed the Moika by a footbridge. She studied the plaques on the houses until she recognized the one with a café a flight up. She remembered the telephone booth in the rear of the café.

She ordered tea with lemon and got up to dial Vera. Ken had always referred to the tiny Ukrainian as "fear-

less Vera"; it took courage to pick them up at the hotel
rather than meet on a street corner. But Vera insisted
that it was the only hospitable thing to do.

"Hello, this is a friend of Andrey's."

"Yes." It was Vera's husband, Tolya. He knew her
voice.

"How are you?"

"Fine."

"Is Vera home?"

"No."

"Will she be home soon?"

"Yes, soon."

"I've come for Andrey's birthday party."

"Yes, I know."

"Are you going there too?"

"Yes."

"Does Vera want to pick me up at the hotel?"

"No. Are you calling from the hotel?"

"Of course not. I'm in a phone booth near the Moika."

"Good."

"Tolya. . . . Shall I. . . . Where can I meet Vera?"

"In the subway station. By the Maryinsky Theater."

"What time?"

"Be there at seven thirty. Inside."

"Fine. Good-bye."

Vannie's hand was trembling when she put the receiver down. She finished her tea and left.

Little Vera was waiting for her near the turnstiles. She
was wearing thin high heels, bringing her up to Vannie's
chin. No handshake, no greeting. Vera put two coins in

the slot, and they took the escalator down. The train rolled gently into the station.

It was crowded. They stood. Vannie bent down and whispered to Vera, "Isn't Tolya coming to Andrey's birthday party?"

"Yes. But later."

"Is something wrong, Vera? Maybe I shouldn't have called you."

"Don't worry. Everything will be all right."

"You're sure?"

Vera smiled. "Oh, things get better, things get worse. We are used to it."

The bus was waiting directly opposite the subway exit. They took seats near the front door. Then Vannie saw Tolya board the bus. A smile already on her face to greet him, Vannie watched as he brushed past them without a word.

"Vera, didn't you see him? Tolya just came on the bus. He's. . . ." Vannie started to turn, but Vera put a hand on hers.

"Don't look back. Tolya likes to go alone. He wanted to make sure that we weren't followed. You know him, Vannie. He is always a little suspicious."

"Not of me?" Vannie protested.

"Of course not. But Tolya likes to be cautious. He's Jewish, after all. He has to be more careful."

At the last stop, Tolya got off first by the rear door. The two women left by the front exit. "But he's walking in the opposite direction!" Vannie exclaimed. Vera merely smiled and assuringly put her arm through hers.

There were no stone paths through the housing development. They walked around the ruts and crossed over a plank of wood that bridged a long, open ditch. Between the gray stucco eggbox buildings, black patches of dying fires scarred the littered gravel; some were still smoking as the last scraps of garbage choked in the embers.

They climbed the two uneven rows of chipped bricks that constituted the front steps of Andrey's house. The hallway light was missing. They walked up a dark concrete staircase to the second floor. The door was open.

A dark-haired friend was sitting cross-legged on the floor, next to a record player. Andrey, wearing his familiar black polo sweater, was stretched out tautly on the living-room daybed, facing the wall, his head tilted toward the music. Vannie could see the rhythmic sway of his arm as it moved ever so slightly to the Bach B Minor Mass. His shoulders tensed as he heard footsteps. He leaped off the bed and ran toward Vannie, bringing both arms tightly around her waist and lifting her off the floor.

"Vannie, Vannie. I knew you would come. You would not disappoint me."

Vannie's eyes were shining. "Andrey, you will never know what it took me to get here. I had to fight half of Moscow."

He put her down, his warm hands holding hers. "Tell me truthfully. Was it worth it?"

"What a question, Andrey! I've come, haven't I?"

"And I am so happy to see you. Especially tonight."

He helped her off with her coat and hung it next to

Vera's behind the front door. "Ken couldn't make it, I see. Well, at least you are here."

"But with Ken's tape recorder." She touched her tote bag.

"Ah, yes. Tonight we record my songs."

"If I can work it. I'm using it for the first time."

"Don't worry, Vannie. If it doesn't go, we push it a little."

He led her toward his dark-haired friend. "You remember Arkim. He brought us fresh wine from Yerevan."

"Oh, I nearly forgot." Vannie ran into the foyer and came back with a small flat package. "Open it, please."

He unwrapped the brown paper and in a little box found a key ring with a medallion of a ram, his zodiac sign. He took out his house key and attached it, murmuring, "It's lovely, lovely. Thank you."

"There's something else, Andrey. In the tissue paper. I hope you like it."

He pulled out an old, sepia-colored photograph of a young woman. "It's my grandmother," Vannie said. "The Russian one."

Andrey collected old photographs. He studied the picture of Vannie's grandmother taken in Kiev more than fifty years ago. His long nose quivered slightly as if he could still smell a young girl's faded scent of jasmine.

"This is marvelous, really marvelous. *Bolshoye spasibo*, Vannie. What a lovely woman she was. You look like her, you know."

"Do you really like the picture, Andrey? You know I never knew her. She died here in Russia during the Civil War. My mother was only a baby when my grandfather took her to America. My mother's thoroughly American. And my father never leaves Binghamton except on business. But when I was a little girl, my grandfather told me about her. He thought I resembled her—she had hair like mine. Maybe that's why I always felt she belonged to me. And if they hadn't left Russia . . . I mean, if there hadn't been a revolution and civil war, maybe I too would have been born in Kiev. I think of it sometimes as a life that might have been."

Andrey nodded, his large brown eyes flecked with sadness. "We, who have remained here, think of it that way too sometimes . . . the life that might have been!"

With an abrupt gesture, Andrey opened his desk drawer and pulled out a sheaf of loose-lying photographs. "Here, look at this one, Vannie. This is *my* grandmother. Now look at yours again. They were both young girls under Nicholas the Second. They never knew each other, but they could be sisters. They are both proud women."

His hand went back in the drawer for more photographs. "Ah, here's my wife's uncle. This was taken during the Civil War. He fought on the side of the Whites. He is so confident they'll win. And this one. These are my parents in 1926. The lake is very near here. These were peaceful days—even after the Revolution. The baby is my older brother—he died during the siege of Leningrad."

Andrey smiled with clenched teeth. "This is my uncle in his Cheka uniform. This is the beginning of Soviet Russia. My uncle was very pleased with himself. Look at his mouth. He helped Stalin purge many 'undesirable' elements in our country. My father's brother! And his photo here, this is his daughter, my cousin! She's no older than you. She is wearing her Komsomol blouse and beret. She looks nothing like my grandmother, nor yours!"

He caressed Vannie's cheek tenderly with the back of his hand. "Nor you, *chère amie.*" Then he put the photographs back in the drawer.

"The Russian face has changed, Vannie. We are different people."

"Not you, Andrey. It is still old Russia when I am back here with you."

He laughed bitterly. "Look at me, Vannie. My grandfather was as tall as Peter the Great. And I am as small as Stalin."

He pulled his friend Arkim by the arm. "Come, no more tonight of the sad fate of Russia. It's my birthday. Let's eat and drink."

The table in the next room was covered with a fresh white cloth. There were two tall silver candlesticks surrounded by plates of salads and smoked meats. At both ends stood decanters of red and white wine. Andrey's wife was carrying a cold bottle of vodka from the kitchen. With her blond softness, she seemed a relic of prerevolutionary days; Andrey complained and enjoyed her.

Vera came and sat between Arkim and a pert-nosed movie actress they called Nadya. Vannie hadn't met her before.

Andrey raised his glass for the first toasts: "To my dearest friends—who are forbidden to leave the table before tomorrow morning." Everyone laughed and started passing plates of fish and herring. With each sip of vodka and then wine, Andrey made another toast. He insisted Nadya eat more potatoes to fatten up for her new movie role. The wine was finished with the grilled lamb. Arkim produced a bottle of sweet champagne from the Crimea while Vera helped Andrey's wife clear the table. When they carried in the glasses of tea and the fruitcake, Arkim brought a guitar to the table, leaning it between Andrey and Vannie.

Andrey raised his glass of champagne. "Before the music, one last toast: to Vannie—and her beautiful grandmother." Vannie closed her eyes lest the tears escape.

While he tuned the guitar, Vannie took out her tape recorder and laid it on the table. She held the microphone, and Andrey began to sing. His voice had a deep, melancholy timbre. He sang simply. Russian folk songs are sad even when the beat is quick and the rhythm gay. Nadya's high soprano joined him in a love duet. Everyone insisted that he play Okudzhava's "Malenki Orkestri," and even Vannie joined in the chorus.

After an hour, Andrey said he was tired. He got up abruptly and put his guitar away. He couldn't be moved to play anymore. Vannie put her tape recorder in her bag—she had used only one track of the cassette.

It was late. The party was over. Time to go home.

"But where is Vera, Andrey?"

"She must have left while we were singing."

"But I wanted to say good-bye to her. And Tolya . . . why didn't Tolya come?"

Andrey's eyes were already half closed. "No, he didn't come, did he? Maybe he doesn't like my music. Who knows?"

He put his hand on Nadya's shoulder. "You'll take Vannie home, won't you?" She nodded, and Andrey walked them to the door for their coats.

"Good-bye, Vannie. My best to Ken. When will you come back to Leningrad to see us?"

She took his hand in hers. "We're leaving soon, Andrey. We're being reassigned this summer, probably to Rome. Maybe someday you'll come see us there."

He dropped her hands. "You're leaving us?" He looked away. "Yes, that's a good one, Vannie. Next year in Rome."

They stood next to each other, saying nothing.

Then he said softly, "*Je suis désolé, tu sais.* But may I keep your grandmother with me in Leningrad?"

"Oh, Andrey, she's all yours." Vannie bent forward and kissed him on the brow. "And Ken and I will listen to your songs in Rome."

He took her hand and kissed the palm.

"Good-bye, Andrey. Good luck."

"Yes, yes. We need luck."

She left the door open and heard him close it slowly behind her.

A vague illumination from the lamppost drifted through the transoms, casting the staircase into striped shadows. Vannie gripped the banister firmly.

"Will you be in Leningrad for long?" Nadya asked, slipping her arm through Vannie's as they descended.

"Just tomorrow. I take the Krasnaya Strela at night back to Moscow."

Nadya sighed. "Oh, how I envy you. I haven't seen Moscow in ages."

"Come with me tomorrow night," Vannie offered. "I'd love to have company on the train."

"I can't, I'm working now. And"—she paused—"it's not a good time to travel."

"Oh, you mean the weather?"

Nadya laughed. "No, no. It is since your radio broadcast about General Zhalkov. We Russians, by instinct, learn to stay home until things quiet down."

Vannie halted on the last step. "You *knew* General Zhalkov?"

Nadya's arm urged her on. "Not personally. But he was a very famous man. A great hero in Leningrad." She untwined her arm from Vannie's to open the front door. "But it is a pity about his nephew, don't you think?"

"You're a friend of Yuri's?" Vannie was stunned.

"We don't have to go around all these houses. By going down this hill, we can reach the street more quickly. Here, give me your hand."

They dug their feet into the soft earth to brake their

speed. At the bottom, they had only to cross an empty lot to reach the main street. Vannie was too agitated to feel the mud oozing into her shoes.

"What do you mean, it was such a pity about Yuri?" Vannie tried to sound casual. "Did something happen to him?"

"I don't know what's happened to him since he went to Moscow. But everyone here says he ruined his career by leaving Leningrad so quickly." She slipped her arm again into Vannie's. "He's very handsome, isn't he? Don't tell me he has broken your heart too?" she chided.

"No, no, he's just a casual friend."

Nadya broke away. Out of the quiet, dimly lit avenue came the bright roof light of an empty taxi. Nadya hailed it and held the door open. "Good-bye, Vannie. It was nice meeting you. I shall ask Andrey for your address when I go to Moscow." She shut the door.

Vannie rolled down the window. "But aren't you coming back to town with me?"

The young actress smiled. "Thank you. I live in another direction. Good night."

Vannie told the driver, "Hotel Astoria." Her fingers fiddled inside her purse. She withdrew an empty package of cigarettes. *Damn, everybody smoked them up.* She crunched the cellophane. *Why did Nadya assume I knew Yuri? God, I want a smoke.* Vannie leaned stiffly against the cold plastic seat as the taxi drove cautiously through the yellow fog.

She had barely opened the door to her suite when the phone rang in the bedroom alcove. The ring was muffled by the closed draperies that divided the two rooms. She dropped her tape recorder and handbag on the chair beside the front door and ran, pushing quickly through the draperies, to the phone beside the bed.

"Hello, hello?" There was no answer. "Hello, who's calling?" She clicked the button up and down. "Who is on the phone?" The line went dead. She put the receiver down and sat on the bed. Then she picked up the phone again.

"Operator . . . operator. Did you call me?"

"No, madame. Didn't you get your party?"

"No, the line went dead."

"Your party must have hung up, madame."

"Yes, I suppose so. Thank you."

She slipped off her coat and then her shoes. That was peculiar. Who could have telephoned at this hour? Alexander Starr? No, he wouldn't call. Who else knew she was here? Andrey? He doesn't have a phone. Probably the KGB making sure she was home and out of mischief. She laughed and, pulling open the red velvet curtains, went back into the living room to close the front door.

"Well, now at least I have Andrey's Russian songs to play in my old age." She picked up the tape recorder and pushed the button down to Play. There was no sound. She opened the case. The cassette was gone.

Chapter Ten

She had locked the door, searched the closets, and even checked under the beds. There was no one else in the room. She was alone. This time she knew. She hadn't dropped it. While she had been decoyed into answering the telephone behind the closed curtains, someone had taken the cassette out of the tape recorder.

Vannie realized that she had been watched from the moment she had arrived in Leningrad. Tolya had not come to the party because she and Vera had been followed out to Andrey's. Vera knew it when Tolya didn't show up by midnight—she had slipped away without even saying good-bye. And Nadya, that great little actress. How did she know that Yuri was a friend of hers? Pure coincidence? And that taxi she hailed—since when do Russian cabs come cruising up out of nowhere at two in the morning?

But why should anyone want to take a cassette of folk songs? It made no sense, but it didn't matter now. She had to get out of Leningrad quickly. She wouldn't wait until the following night for the Krasnaya Strela. The Intourist office would be open by eight. She would buy a plane ticket and fly back to Moscow that morning. Still dressed, she lay on the bed and dozed until dawn broke.

She fought with Intourist for two hours. First they pretended there were no planes to Moscow that day. Then, there was a plane, but it had already left. The next one was fully booked. Besides, they wouldn't let her take it because she was scheduled to leave by train. Finally she started to scream: "You can't keep me here because of your regulations. I don't give a damn about your regulations. It takes five minutes to cancel my train reservation. If there's no seat on the plane, just give me standby. I'm not upsetting your schedule. I planned to leave before midnight, and now all I want is to leave a few hours earlier."

She opened her wallet and took out her rubles and dollars. "I'm perfectly willing to pay the difference in price in whatever currency you want."

"What's the matter, Vannie? Are you trying to buy something again with your American dollars?"

Beside Vannie stood Michael Petrov. He was carrying a Samsonite suitcase and had his black trenchcoat draped over his arm.

"Yes, I am. And I haven't met the Russian yet who will refuse them. I want to get on the next plane to Moscow."

"That shouldn't be so hard to arrange. I am leaving on it myself."

"Well, I've been standing here for two hours and haven't got a straight answer yet."

He looked at his watch. "There's a little time yet. Wait here. Give me your ticket and passport."

She pushed her passport and train tickets toward him. Stuffing her rubles and dollars back into her wallet, she placed it on top of her travel papers. "Here, take it all. It's all I have left. Just please get me out of here."

"I'll be back in a few minutes," he said. Leaving his suitcase beside hers, he walked through a small door marked Private. *Have things come to such a pass that Michael Petrov is now in charge of my travel arrangements?* she mused.

Petrov returned before Vannie had finished her cigarette. "It will take ten minutes. The plane leaves at noon. Come, I'll buy you a vodka while we're waiting." Vannie pointed toward the suitcases. "Don't worry," he said, amused, "nobody will steal them." He turned to the Intourist girl. "Have a taxi waiting in fifteen minutes to go to the airport." He led Vannie to the restaurant bar.

"*Odnu vodku, odin tomatni sok,*" he ordered.

"Aren't you going to have a vodka too?"

"I don't drink."

Damn his beard, Vannie thought. *It hides his mouth.*

The bartender poured their drinks. Petrov raised his glass of tomato juice. "To Soviet-American friendship." Vannie nodded, said nothing, and downed her vodka in one swallow.

He watched her. "Are you upset?" he asked.

"Why should I be upset? I've just been tailed every minute of the twenty-four hours that I've been in Leningrad."

"That's perfectly normal, Vannie. Do you think Russians are not followed when they leave Washington for Chicago?"

"You always have a ready answer, Michael. Do Russian tourists in Chicago also have their tape recorders stolen?"

"Was your tape recorder stolen?" He was surprised.

"No, but my cassette was—that was inside it."

"What was on the cassette?"

"Just some simple Russian folk songs that a friend of mine sang at his birthday party."

"You mean this?" Michael Petrov held a cassette in his hand.

"Do you mean you took. . . ."

"I took nothing." His voice was edgy. "It was borrowed from you last night, and it is I who am returning it." He looked at her and smiled. "If it belongs to you, take it."

She reached for it tentatively, almost expecting him to take it back. She fingered it while he paid the check. "Come, put it away. Your ticket must be in order by now."

They rode together out to the airport. Vannie had her cassette, a hard knot in her stomach, and a million questions that he didn't seem to want to answer.

"Are you one of the foreigners who prefer Leningrad to Moscow?" he asked.

"Yes. And are you one of those Muscovites who feel Leningrad is just a provincial town?"

"But it's true. It is very pretty, and it has its charm. And for foreigners it is a little bit of old Europe. It should be. It was built by Italians. But Russia has only one capital."

"For you only Moscow counts," she snapped. "Leningrad can be left to die a provincial death."

"Don't be so angry, Vannie. You foreigners become so partisan—as if Leningrad belonged to you. I, too, am very fond of this city. That is precisely why I am here now." He gazed out the window, slowly stroking his beard. "Pity your husband is in London. If he cared as much about Leningrad as I do. . . ."

"Good Lord," she interrupted, "you mean you too think. . . ."

"I try to think as little as possible, Vannie. But I do know a few things. And so do you. More than you realize. Do you have everything? The airport is right around the bend."

It was a Finnair flight, and the plane was late. As soon as it took off from Helsinki, there would be an announcement, they said. Petrov led Vannie to the buffet—a small, stand-up snack bar. "You see, the restaurant at Sheremetyevo Airport in Moscow is far more cosmopolitan." He ordered sausages and coffee, and they carried them to a small Formica table wedged between two plastic armchairs.

"What did you start to say, Michael, about my husband not caring about Leningrad?"

"Let us say he is indifferent. His story that General Zhalkov was assassinated by a captain in his command will cause irreparable harm here."

"Now just wait a minute. Ken never wrote that story."

"Yes, he did, Vannie. He passed the story on to a colleague so that, he hoped, it couldn't be traced to him. But the information was given to him in Moscow." He took a bite of the crinkled sausage. "It was you, Vannie, who carried the message to him."

"You are out of your mind."

Petrov didn't answer.

Then suddenly, Vannie remembered. The single sheet of onionskin paper. She had hidden it from consciousness from the moment it had dropped out of her bag when they had come home from Rabichov's cocktail party. Ken had picked it up. He had tucked it in his pocket. And he had left Moscow the next day.

"I can see by your face that your memory is returning."

"But how do you know about it?" Vannie whispered.

"Because, my dear Vannie, I know who slipped it into your shopping bag."

"FINNAIR FLIGHT 742 TO MOSCOW BOARDING IMMEDIATELY. GATE TWO. LAST CALL. LAST CALL."

Her sausage uneaten, their coffee barely sipped, Vannie and Petrov were the last to board the plane. There were no two seats together. He said that they would talk later. But Vannie wondered where and when. The moment seemed gone.

Petrov had his Triumph waiting in the parking lot at Sheremetyevo. "Are you expecting your car, Vannie?"

"No one is expecting me."

"Fine, come have lunch with me."

The car was cold. She huddled against the door, tucking her chin into her fur collar.

"It will warm up in a few minutes," he assured her. "The British heater wasn't very good. I've just had a new German one installed."

"East or West German?" she asked archly.

Petrov smiled. "Does it make a difference to you, really? It doesn't to me. I simply buy the best heater on the market."

"Provided, of course, you have Western currency."

He was thoughtful for a moment. "No, buying the best is more a matter of taste than money."

Damn it, thought Vannie, *English is my language and he always seems to have the last word.*

It had snowed in Moscow the day before, yet the road was clear. Snow clearing in Moscow was a marvel. If there were a freak snowstorm in July, the snowplow army of Soviet womanhood and the broom brigade of babushkas could be mobilized within minutes.

Yet the snow rested heavily on the birches and the pine branches. Suddenly she sat erect. They were driving deeper into the countryside, away from Moscow.

"Where are we going, Michael?"

"To my place."

"But your apartment is in town!"

"Yes, you and Ken have been there. It's very convenient for entertaining."

"Then why are we taking the road to Peredelkino?"

"Because that is where my dacha is," he answered calmly. "Don't be alarmed, Vannie. The road is not slippery. Or do you think I am kidnapping you?"

"No, no," she said quickly. "I just didn't know that you had a dacha."

"Every Russian has one. Even if it is only his cousin's unheated, one-room—how do you call it—shack?"

"You, Michael Petrov, have a shack." Vannie laughed.

He was serious. "You will see it in a few minutes."

They drove past the village church, near the summer residence of the Moscow Patriarch. The road was winding up, but not sharply, and there were no other cars. Little houses with gingerbread shutters peeped out from among the trunks of towering evergreens. It was all white today, as in deepest winter. Down a steep incline was Michael Petrov's two-car garage.

The dacha was a sprawling clapboard villa halfway up the hill. They climbed the wide terrace steps already cleared of snow. Smoke drifted up from the chimney, and an old woman's face looked out from a bay window.

"You see over there, Vannie. That's my skating rink."

"Did you invite me out here to go ice skating?"

"If you like. It's very pleasant after a big lunch."

The face that observed them from the window reappeared behind the front door. "This is my babushka," Michael explained. "Actually she was an old friend of my mother's. She and her husband keep the house and grounds in order for me."

"*Obed*, Mamushka, we are starving." The old lady waddled off into the kitchen.

The living room was dark. The branches of the birch trees crossing in front of the windows obscured the daylight. There was a fire going on the hearth, and above it, protected from the heat by a marble mantelpiece, was Petrov's collection of rare icons.

"Nothing more modern than the seventeenth century," he said. "The red and gold one on the top row is from the fourteenth. I picked it up last year in Novgorod."

Bookcases lined both sides of the fireplace, and tucked in at shoulder level was a stereo hi-fi. "Would you like some music?" he offered.

Vannie nodded. She studied the room: the Queen Anne settees, the Chippendale tables, the chintz curtains. It was an English squire's country estate!

"May I give you a Pimm's? Or would you prefer a Coca-Cola?"

"Just a tomato juice, thank you."

On the coffee table were copies of the *Economist*, the *New Yorker*, and *Town and Country*. In the bookshelves, alongside volumes of Marx and Lenin, were Trotsky's memoirs and Churchill's histories. Petrov came back with two glasses of tomato juice.

"How do you get all these books and magazines? I've never seen them in a Russian home before. I thought they were forbidden."

"I ordered them by mail. Come finish your drink. Lunch is ready."

Petrov was preoccupied as he ate. He asked her once if she would like some more blinis and caviar. She told him

the stew was delicious and so was the ice cream. If he
didn't want to talk, why had he invited her out?

"I would love to try your ice rink, Michael," she said,
"but I'm afraid I didn't bring my skates."

He beamed. "Would you really? I have many pairs of
ice skates. Come into the foyer. They are all black. I
know that American women like white ones. But there
should be a pair to fit you."

Dressed again, they walked down to the smooth iced
clearing, and Petrov helped her off with her boots.
"Aren't you going to skate?" Vannie asked.

"I don't skate," he said somberly.

She felt foolish all by herself, gliding and turning, a
lone dancer on a white floor. But after a few minutes,
when her fe warmed, she started to hum and cut figure
eights. After a quarter of an hour, she glided back to
Petrov.

"It was nice watching you. You enjoy skating." He
carried her skates up the path. "Come, let's leave them in
the house and go for a walk. These are all my woods back
here."

There was a trail behind the dacha leading to a small
wooden bridge and then up toward the top of the hill.
They walked beside each other, gloved hands dug deeply
into their pockets. The path was firm, and the fresh snow
crunched under their boots. Vannie wanted Petrov to
begin. But he didn't.

"Thank you for returning the cassette, Michael."

"I'm happy to be of service. Be sure you don't leave it
lying around again."

"I didn't. It was just that the phone. . . . But why were they keeping tabs on me constantly? In the subway, in the taxi?"

"Everyone coming and going to Leningrad these days is being followed closely."

"Just because of Ken's story about the Zhalkov assassination?"

"Don't give yourself airs, Vannie. Foreign correspondents aren't that important in the Soviet Union."

"Obviously someone at Sasha Rabichov's thought Ken was important enough to take the story out." Vannie was annoyed.

"Important people are never invited to Sasha Rabichov's cocktail parties. They are strictly bait for diplomatic minnows. And your husband swallowed the bait —as you say—hook, line, and sinker."

"The story wasn't true?"

"It is far more serious than 'not true.' You and your husband were used to whitewash a murder."

"That's impossible!" Vannie was indignant. "Neither Ken nor I have ever had anything to do with Army people."

"I see there's no point explaining it. You are children. You will never understand what you have done."

"Let me try and understand, please. General Zhalkov really was murdered, wasn't he?"

"Do you care? Does the name mean anything to you, Vannie? Had you ever heard of him before he became a front-page story?"

"Well. . . . I. . . . He was military attaché in Rome, I believe."

"Very good, Vannie. *Brava.* You learned that from Ambassador Succioli, no doubt. Is that all he told you about him?"

"That's all I remember," she said.

"You wish *me* to talk? Very well. Let me continue your education then. Last August, when the decision was made to march into Czechoslovakia, it was General Zhalkov who was designated to lead the troops. He refused. Do you know what that means?"

"He was a very brave man."

"Yes, but that's irrelevant. For many people in the Kremlin, Zhalkov became an enemy, a potential leader of opposition. One does not refuse a command. And one does not talk about it to colleagues."

"Well, why didn't you arrest Zhalkov right away?"

Petrov turned on her angrily. "Whom do you mean by 'you'?"

Vannie hesitated a minute. "The KGB, the secret police, of course."

"Then do not look at me and say 'you.' I do not arrest people. And I do not work for the KGB."

"I'm sorry. I didn't mean you personally. It was just a manner of speaking."

His face relaxed. "All right, then. Shall we continue our little seminar on Soviet politics?"

"Please don't talk to me like a child, Michael. I have simply grown up in a country where life . . . where politics is not so complicated. But I have lived here nearly two years. I have tried . . . very hard, to understand. And I have learned that when you . . . I mean when the Soviet authorities think someone is dangerous, they find a way of getting rid of him."

"Excellent, Vannie. That is, generally speaking, correct. But General Zhalkov was too important to be simply eliminated. So an effort was made to get him to confess his 'mistake.' The KGB arrived one night to take him away for questioning."

"He refused to admit he was wrong?"

"They never got as far as that. They never even got him out of his apartment. He was murdered in his own living room."

"How do you know all this?"

"We have a tape. A recording of the KGB's fiasco. The night they arrived at Zhalkov's. His struggle. His death."

Vannie's breath came in short gasps. "So the KGB put out the story that a captain in Zhalkov's command murdered him. That way the KGB cleared itself by blaming it on the Army."

"Exactly. If the Army had learned *why* the KGB wanted to get rid of Zhalkov, who can predict how various officers would have reacted? He was very popular among his men."

"So planting the murder on an Army officer covers up the political implications as well," she said.

"It goes even beyond that. If one officer murders an-

147

other, everyone suspects an Army plot. And the KGB has a perfectly legitimate excuse to clear out other so-called undesirable elements in the Army."

"But, Michael, that could lead to a whole purge. It would be going back to Stalin's time." Vannie was aghast.

"Yes, it would," Petrov said dryly.

"But if the KGB had their alibi, why did they have to slip it into my shopping bag? What difference does it make to them what the foreign press thinks?"

"Your foreign press, Vannie, is also a tool for the KGB. When an important story gets into the Western press, it is beamed back into the Soviet Union through the BBC and the Voice of America. And for millions of Russians with shortwave radios, who listen to them every day, your stations carry more truth than a thousand issues of *Pravda*."

"But who slipped the fake story into my bag?"

"That is for your husband to tell you," he said.

"I'm sure he didn't know. Really, we had no way of knowing."

"Very few people did. Even now. There are many people who suspect. But there are no more than . . . perhaps two dozen people in the Soviet Union who know what I have told you this afternoon."

"But Yuri, General Zhalkov's nephew, did he know?"

"Know? Precisely? I don't think so. He came by to have breakfast with his uncle the morning after the murder. It was he who found the body. The KGB has been giving him a hard time ever since. They got him dismissed from his job in Leningrad. That wasn't too difficult. He had a record of being a troublemaker. He signed a petition last year protesting the march into Czechoslovakia."

"My God," Vannie wailed. "I never knew anything. But, Michael, why have you told me all this?"

"I don't know, Vannie. Perhaps because we are in the woods. Because it is only when walking like this in the snow that one feels free to talk." He smiled. "Perhaps that is why we Russians like to take so many walks in the woods. It is good for our ulcers." He took off his glasses and pinched the bridge of his nose. "Come, I am tired. Let's go back."

The trees looked black now. The sky and the snow blended in grays. She touched his arm. "Michael, before we're back in the dacha . . . is there something I can do? Maybe something I could tell Ken. Something? Anything?"

He looked down at his boots and kicked a little snow. "Perhaps. I'll think about it. Let's have some tea first."

It was nearly dark when the two of them crossed the wooden bridge and went back into the dacha. The samovar in the living room steamed with boiling water, and a small pot of strong tea was placed on top to keep warm. On the tray beside the samovar was a plate of honey cakes and two empty glasses in silver holders.

"Would you prefer a cup?"

"No, I like my tea in a glass. No lemon, just sugar."

149

"Let's take it in my study. It's warmer there. My housekeeper thinks it's wasteful to keep the fire going all day in this big room."

Vannie carried the plate of honey cakes and put it on the table in front of the leather sofa. After settling down with her tea, she looked above Petrov's desk. There, between two windows, hung the small Fontanova oil painting that she had seen and loved at Sasha Rabichov's cocktail party.

"Do you still like it, Vannie?"

"Yes, very much."

"Well, then take it." He lifted the unframed, wood-backed canvas from the wall and held it out to her.

"Don't be silly, I just can't take a painting like that."

"Why not?"

"I just can't. That's all. It's not right."

"You Americans are so suspicious of what you don't pay for. Would you like to give me one large silver dollar for it? Would that make you feel better?"

"No, it's not that."

"Then take it. It's already yours."

He leaned it against the sofa as she sipped her tea. Then he went over to the desk, picked up the telephone, and started to dial. "I hope you don't mind if I don't drive you home. I'll call a taxi. Is that all right?"

She nodded and quickly finished her tea. She put on her coat and boots and he handed her the Fontanova.

"Here, you hold the painting. I'll carry your suitcase out to the taxi."

Halfway down the steps she stopped.

"Michael, what shall I say to Ken?"

"That I gave you the painting as a gift."

"No, I mean about . . . everything else."

"Why must you say anything?"

"Because he is coming back tomorrow."

"Really? Well, I wouldn't say anything. I would just leave the Soviet Union as soon as possible."

"Leave? Why?"

"Because you know too much, and somebody might find out how much." He opened the door of the taxi. Vannie got in, and he handed the driver her suitcase. "Forget all this unpleasantness, Vannie. Leave Moscow and take your music with you. Listen to your Russian folk songs. They will last longer than all of us. *Do svidanya.*"

The taxi lumbered through Peredelkino until it hit the Minsk highway. Then it sped along the dark road, avoiding the icy shoulders.

Chapter Eleven

Snow fell lightly that night as the temperature dropped below zero. Vannie awoke next morning to the rumbling of cold motors in the courtyard. She glanced at the clock. Ken's secretary would arrive in an hour. On returning from Petrov's dacha, Vannie had phoned Alla to arrange an appointment at the Tretyakov Gallery for this morning. She had decided to declare her paintings officially and to ask the Tretyakov for the clearance required by customs.

Should she declare the Fontanova as well? Petrov's gift, the smiling girl in beige with half-closed eyes, was perched on her dressing table, awaiting her decision. If she declared it with the others, she would have to explain how she had got it. Under no circumstances did she wish to be so closely linked with Petrov. The Fontanova was small—perhaps small enough to be taken out in her hand luggage, which customs rarely examined.

The telephone beside the bed startled her.

"Madame Tomkins? One minute please. Rome calling."

Vannie's mind raced: What could she tell Ken—that his Zhalkov story was a fake, a plant? But Petrov might have been wrong. Perhaps Ken had not been in London.

How could she even hint about it on the open telephone line?

"Vannie, where the devil have you been? I tried to get you all evening." Ken's voice was clear—none of the usual local static; the call was being monitored directly.

"I was visiting. Nothing important. You'll be home tomorrow?"

"That's what I'm calling about. Are you sitting down?"

"I'm still in bed."

"I'm not coming back at all. I can't. The Soviet embassy called me yesterday. They've canceled my reentry visa. . . . Hello? Are you still there?"

"I'm here."

"Speak louder. I can't hear you."

"Then you can't come back to Moscow? Ever?"

"Don't take it so hard, Vannie. There's good news, too. London is our next assignment."

"You were in London?"

"Just for a couple of days. The London office looks great. Vannie? Can you hear me? Aren't you delighted with the news?"

"Yes, yes, I hear you very well. But what reason did they give you? Why aren't they letting you back in?"

"Who knows? They never explain anything. We'll talk about it when you get out. Get your visa today and take Alitalia out tomorrow."

"I can't, Ken. Not that quickly."

"Why not? Let Alla or Nancy pack the trunk after you've gone."

"It's not that. I still have to say good-bye to friends. And my paintings . . . I'm going to the Tretyakov. . . ."

"Forget about those paintings, will you please? Just exit fast. Cable me which plane you'll take. I'll meet you at Fiumicino Airport." He hung up.

Vannie's hand rested on the phone. Petrov was right: Ken had carried out the fake Zhalkov story and even gone to London to plant it. Was that why the Russians had canceled his reentry visa?

She would have to leave quickly now—in a day, two at most. She had to see Yuri and Lydia. But how could she get to Lydia's studio without being followed? And her paintings—were they worth the trouble? Were they of any artistic value whatever? Perhaps not, but Vannie couldn't let go of them, any of them. Like the cassette with Andrey's songs and her little red address book, the paintings were her Russian life.

She heard the front-door key turn, as Alla let herself into the apartment. Vannie quickly snatched the Fontanova and slipped it under the bedcovers.

Alla entered the bedroom, with her raccoon coat hanging around her narrow shoulders like an oversized blanket, her wet boots dripping on the rug. "You're still in your nightgown? You have an appointment at the Tretyakov in half an hour. Ivan is downstairs warming up the car."

"I'll be ready in a few minutes. Come, Alla, sit here on the bed. I have to tell you something. Ken just called. He's not coming back. His reentry visa has been canceled."

Alla's hand fluttered to her mouth. "There will be a new correspondent here?"

"I suppose so. My goodness, Alla, after ten years and four different bosses, you should be used to it."

"I get used to everything, in time. But I don't like changes." She looked at Vannie furtively. "Why did they cancel his visa?"

"He didn't tell me."

Alla sucked in her lips as if savoring a lemon. "They probably won't let me work for foreigners anymore."

"Don't be silly, Alla. What has one thing to do with another?"

"For you, nothing. But for me, it's a bad mark against my name. Never mind. You don't understand the mentality here." Wearily Alla got up from the bed. "You get dressed, Vannie. I'll make some coffee."

"All right. Oh, by the way, Alla, did you see a red address book lying on the dining-room table when I was in Leningrad?"

"It was with your ticket and passport. You took it with you. Why?"

"Nothing important. I must have left it on the train. There wouldn't be any way of getting it back, would there? Calling Helsinki, maybe?"

"I'll call the Leningrad Station later. Maybe they found it." Alla went into the kitchen to prepare coffee.

When Vannie heard the water running, she crept noiselessly into the storage closet. Unlocking the trunk, pushing aside her ski clothes, she lifted out the two large paintings to take to the Tretyakov. In their place, she slipped the Fontanova. Then she locked the trunk.

They entered the Tretyakov Gallery by the side entrance. The "judgment room," one flight up, was palatial, with a high baroque ceiling and tall bay windows. Grave nineteenth-century portraits hung from the gilt-trimmed wall panels. Vannie sat with Alla on a wooden bench as a chunky, gray-haired curator in a musty wool dress studied the two abstract paintings propped up on the marble mantelpiece.

The public rooms of the Tretyakov overflowed with acceptable Russian art, ranging from twelfth-century mosaic icons to contemporary murals of red-cheeked factory workers. For the Tretyakov to declare two underground abstract paintings "national treasures" would be the height of irony. And, according to the Soviet rules, a painting not considered a "national treasure" could be legally taken out of the country. It sounded logical.

The curator studied and measured the paintings. She asked Vannie from whom she had bought them and how much she had paid. Vannie said that both paintings had been gifts from the artists, so that there would be no question of illegal currency transactions. A colleague was called in, an elderly gentleman with a white goatee; the two museum officials conferred in hushed tones. After a few minutes, he left, nodding pleasantly to Vannie.

"You may take your paintings, Mrs. Tomkins," the curator announced.

Vannie shot Alla a look of triumph. "Then you don't regard them as national treasures?"

"We have no interest in them." She returned to her desk angled in the corner by the bay window.

Vannie followed her. "I may be leaving the country tomorrow. Don't I need a special stamp from you to get them through customs?"

"That is not our domain. To take them out of the Soviet Union, you will need permission from the Ministry of Culture. I shall inform them of your request."

"But what do I do now? Should I bring the paintings over there?"

"That will not be necessary. They do not wish to see them. Their decision is based on other factors." She pointed to the canvases. "You may take them with you now. The Ministry of Culture will notify you tomorrow."

Ivan was waiting for them downstairs. As he lay each painting carefully in the car trunk, Alla told Vannie she couldn't ride back with them, murmuring something about a lunch date on the Arbat. She promised to be back at two o'clock.

Driving into the compound, Ivan suddenly remembered a meeting of Special Service chauffeurs for which he was already late. Could he take the car?

Damn, damn, damn, thought Vannie as she plodded up the stairs herself, dragging a nontreasure under each arm. *Can't anyone in this country ever simply say, "I have to report to the police" without all these elaborate excuses?*

Vannie fixed herself a caviar sandwich and a pot of coffee in the kitchen and brought it to the other side of the apartment, setting down the tray on the recessed window ledge in the living room. It was drizzling. She watched last night's snow turn gray and melt black on the tarred roadway.

With the first swallow of hot coffee, she spotted the new militiaman in the courtyard. She put her cup down and watched his march beneath her window. He took thirty paces toward the fence. Then he turned and took thirty paces back toward the main militia box. He turned again. Thirty paces. Fence. Turn. March. He was patrolling Vannie's entrance!

"You bastards!" she said aloud. "Now you're giving me your private protection."

Spellbound, she watched him pace. Square shoulders, navy blue uniform, high black boots, brown leather holster slung around his hips. He would lean against the railing as a car went by. Then he would continue to pace.

She ran to get her cigarettes from the foyer. When she rehoisted herself on the living-room window ledge, the special militiaman had crossed the center yard. He posted himself in front of the opposite entrance and looked straight up at Vannie's window. When he saw her, he crossed back. He marched again under her window. Thirty paces. The minutes passed and then an hour.

Vannie went into the kitchen to empty an ashtray. She stared mindlessly out of the kitchen window at the mud mounds and stray beer bottles that littered the forty feet between the back of her building and the back fence.

Then she saw a black mongrel burrow a hole under the high mesh wire fence. The dog finally arched its back and escaped the compound. Vannie's eyes lit up. "Good doggie!" She ran back to the living room, looked out, and waited.

At two o'clock, Ivan drove the big, black Impala into the courtyard. He passed her entrance and parked the car between the two buildings. He got out and opened the hood. The militiaman joined him. Ivan poked his hand into the motor while the militiaman watched. They talked. Ivan smiled. It was so simple, as though they were chatting about the merits of an American generator. Then Ivan closed the hood, dutifully locked the car, and entered Vannie's building.

She slipped off the ledge and opened the door. Ivan stood there, pleased as a peacock.

"I want to get gas, gospozha."

"Not now, Ivan. Alla will be here any minute. You'll drive her to the Ministry of Foreign Affairs."

"But we may not have enough gas to get there, gospozha."

"I thought the rule was to have at least a quarter tank at all times."

Ivan giggled. "But the gauge is broken, gospozha. I don't know how much we have."

"Is that what you were discussing with the militiaman, Ivan?"

"What militiaman?"

"Never mind."

"Oh, him? Downstairs? He's an old neighbor of mine."

"I see. I wasn't sure." Vannie started to close the door. "Ivan, drive the car over to the office, please. Alla will find you there."

"As you like, gospozha. When Gospodin Tomkins is not here, you are my commander."

Vannie brought her coat and bag to the living-room window ledge. Below, Ivan smiled to the militiaman. Then he drove to the far side of the courtyard near Ken's office.

Thirty paces. Vannie lit another cigarette. Turn. "I'll get out of this prison if it's the last thing I do." Thirty paces. She looked at her watch. It was nearly two thirty. Turn.

He walked past the corner of the building toward the fence. Twenty-nine, thirty. Turn. March. Past her entrance. Twenty-nine, thirty. This time he didn't turn. He continued to walk toward the main militia box at the far end of the compound. How long would she have before he turned around again? Thirty seconds or a minute?

She grabbed her coat and bag and flew down the two flights. She slipped out the front door, barely opening it. Then, pressing her back against the building façade, she sidestepped along the top stair, jumped off at the corner, and ran along the side of the building toward the back fence. She paused a second. "Where did that dog get out?" Then she remembered; it was just to the right of her kitchen window.

First she tugged at the mesh fence—it wouldn't budge. Then she tried to bend back the sharp, iron threads at the bottom; she cut her thumb. She crouched low and started to crawl through on her knees. A sharp edge caught her between the shoulder blades. She stretched her legs out behind her, her shoes cutting a backward path through a melting snow mound. Lying flat on the ground, she pulled herself through on the palms of her hands. Once her body had cleared the fence, she stretched her arm under again to pull out her coat and bag.

She crossed the street quickly and darted into a muddy alleyway between two rows of wooden shacks, emerging on Vorovsky Boulevard. She slipped into the first dark vestibule and leaned against the wall. A few people passed. No one looked in. *I made it, you bastards.* She brushed the dirt off the front of her dress and legs. Then she dried her hands in the lining of her coat. The sweat on the back of her neck was turning cold. She slipped on her coat and turned up the collar. Then she casually left the vestibule and walked slowly toward the Kiev railroad station.

Two endless waiting rooms were strewn with families of peasants curled up on the floor. Vannie picked her way carefully, avoiding the sleeping heads and empty milk bottles. Finally, just before the public toilets, she found a phone booth. It reeked of unflushed waters. Holding her breath, she deposited two kopecks and dialed. After several minutes, a familiar voice answered. Vannie hung up.

It had started to drizzle again as she crossed the bridge leading to the Arbat. It was Lydia who had answered the phone. She was home.

Chapter Twelve

Vannie was about to knock. She abruptly halted the gesture and placed her hand over her chest. Her heart was pounding. From one trap into another, she thought. Turning the knob noiselessly, she darted in, tiptoeing along the corridor. Pausing a moment in front of Lydia's studio, she listened for voices. Then slowly she pushed the door ajar.

In the slit of dusty light that parted the dark shadows of the basement room, Lydia sat motionless, her eyes closed. The broken ceramic had been swept away. The few small pieces of bronze sculpture that survived were arranged in clusters along the open shelves. The studio seemed orderly again, as if nothing had ever disturbed its calm. But for Vannie, the tranquillity of Lydia's studio had fled, as she had eight days ago.

Lydia's eyes opened wide. Then, seeing it was Vannie, she rushed up from her chair to embrace her. Leaning her head on Vannie's shoulder, she murmured, "I'm so, so glad to see you."

"You are all right, aren't you, Lydia?"

"Oh, Vannie, I didn't know if you would ever come

back to us. Wait here, just a minute. Let me fill the kettle. Then we can talk."

Vannie stood alone in the middle of the square room. She heard only the running water from the sink in the corridor. What if the KGB came back now? How could she escape? The window separating the basement studio from the street pavement was barred by iron grillwork.

Lydia returned and lit the primus stove. She left the kettle to boil as she gathered her tea things and brought them to the desk.

"Where are Yuri's stones?" Vannie asked.

Lydia hesitated. "He gave them to a friend."

"Then he doesn't come here anymore?"

"Yes, yes. He'll be back in a few minutes. Please take off your coat. Yuri will be very happy to see you."

"I really don't have time to stay," Vannie said.

Lydia nodded. "I understand," she said quietly.

"All right. But just one cup. Then I must go."

Vannie watched Lydia as she fetched the steaming kettle. *Yes, let's have a tea party*, she thought. *Let's pretend nothing happened. All very civilized. No searches. No thugs. No memories.*

"Lydia, what will you do now?"

"I don't know."

"What about your sculpture? You're going to start again, aren't you?"

"Perhaps."

"But you must," Vannie insisted.

"Why? One cannot push things."

"It's not because of the KGB, is it? You don't expect them back?"

Lydia smiled, faintly surprised. "Of course. One always expects them. Don't look so horrified. I try not to think of it. At least not all the time."

"Oh, Lydia, how can you live like that?"

The frail young Russian shrugged her shoulders. "I've never known any other way, Vannie. That's what our life is all about—what we do while we wait. The little compromises we make, such little ones, in the hope of postponing their knock on the door. If we are lucky, we are not home when they come."

"But why you? You've never done anything wrong."

"Who can say what is right? It changes so often in our country." Lydia touched Vannie's cheek gently. "No, you don't understand, do you? Perhaps it is just because you don't understand that we love you. When you come to us, we talk about painting and Chekhov, and you think we are like normal people everywhere. And that we want to believe too, very much."

"But before Yuri . . . until his uncle was killed, the KGB never bothered you?"

Lydia poured the tea and added hot water from the kettle. "Vannie, in all the time you've been here, have you ever wondered how I earned my permit to live in Moscow? How I keep this precious little studio off the Arbat? I have no job. Why am I not expelled from this city as a parasite?"

"But you sold a large bust of Lenin a few months ago."

Lydia nodded. "Yes, those are the little rewards—they buy a bust that looks like a thousand others, that almost anyone could do. But I'm not speaking of money. I'm talking about the privilege of surviving in this city. Why am I free to invite a foreigner—you—to come sit for me?"

Vannie stammered. "What are you trying to say to me?"

"No, no, *dorogaya*. I am not an informer. I don't rush to volunteer information. I don't arrange meetings and set traps. I am not Sasha Rabichov. I shall never earn a trip to Paris. But when they ask me, Vannie, I cannot deny that you come to my studio. If I did, I could never see you again." She paused. "Are you ashamed of me?"

Vannie shook her head violently. "No, no, Lydia, how can I be? If I were in your place, who knows what I would do? Remember last week, when the KGB was here. The stupid things I said . . . and all the other things I should have said."

Lydia placed her hand on Vannie's arm. "What could you have said or done? It was so painful for you . . . to see us as we really are. I wish there had been a way of warning you. . . ."

Vannie felt a draft behind her and turned quickly. Yuri stood in the doorway, very tall, pale, more surprised than pleased. He hung his leather jacket on the hook behind the door and switched on the overhead light. "I didn't think you would come back here, Vannie," he said. "Were you afraid?"

"Yes."

"Are you still?"

Vannie glanced up again at the barred window. "Yes."

Yuri pulled a loaf of bread and a package of cheese from his briefcase and brought it to the table. Gripping the bread firmly, he sliced it. He unpeeled a triangle of cheese and offered it to Vannie. She shook her head.

"Have some," he insisted gently. "They won't be back today."

"How do you know?"

Yuri poured himself a glass of tea. "You embarrassed them last time. They weren't expecting you. Next time, they'll make sure I'm alone."

"They're going to search the studio again?"

"Perhaps." He refilled Vannie's teacup.

"But they won't arrest you?"

He shrugged his shoulders. "They might." He pulled up a chair and sat opposite Vannie, next to Lydia.

"But then how can you sit here drinking tea? So calmly, as if nothing happened."

Yuri looked up. "Why shouldn't we eat and drink? It's perfectly normal. What would you have us do—hide under the bed?"

"Anything," she burst out, "but just not sit here and wait for them. Can't you go away?"

Yuri put his glass down. "Go where, Vannie? There's no place to hide in this country. We try to hide behind our masks, conceal our thoughts, our feelings—but you can't do that forever. We must take off our masks sometimes, to know we are still human."

"But everyone has to conceal his real feelings sometimes, not just here."

"Maybe. Maybe it's a great luxury anywhere to wear your own face. But here, once *they* have seen it, you can't hide it ever again."

He offered Vannie a Russian cigarette and lit it. Vannie wondered if he realized how marvelously handsome he was. His eyes, as on the day she had first met him, before all the trouble, were still so clear, a luminous blue.

"Yuri . . . tell me . . ." she began, and then glanced furtively around the room.

"Are you looking for the microphones, Vannie?" he asked. "They've put them in the overhead lamp."

"Can't you disconnect them?"

"That would only annoy them. They'd come back that much sooner." Lydia moved her chair back, permitting Yuri to withdraw a transistor radio from the table drawer. He found a station playing Cossack dances and turned it up loud enough to blanket their voices.

"Why do they want to arrest you, Yuri? You haven't committed any crime."

"Nobody is innocent in this country, Vannie. They could arrest me on several charges. I'm here in Moscow without a residence permit, and I don't have a job. That makes me a social parasite, legally speaking."

"But you could find a job. You have a profession."

"Nobody will hire me, Vannie. I've tried. I can't get a job laying bricks. I've sold the stones. That's what we're living on."

"But why, Yuri? Why are they hunting you?"

He rose and walked over toward the window, staring out at the patch of sidewalk. Children's feet skipped past the iron grillwork.

"Vannie, do you know why my uncle was killed?"

She was hesitant. Was this the moment for telling him of her talk with Petrov? "Well . . . I've heard it's because he wouldn't lead the troops into Czechoslovakia."

Yuri shook his head. "No, that was only the beginning. If it had just been his refusal, he would have been forced to retire in disgrace, maybe had his pension cut off. He was prepared for that. The real danger came months later."

Yuri was standing directly under the microphones. Vannie turned the dial, making the music louder, snatches of the *Firebird Suite*. Realizing that Vannie had turned up the volume to blanket his voice, he moved away, settling down on the floor with cigarettes and ashtray, his back against the front door.

"Several officers in my uncle's command came to see him when they got back from Czechoslovakia. They'd been told that they were giving 'fraternal aid.' Instead, they found a whole people hating them. They were spat on. Women and children cried at the mere sight of them. They didn't understand. One by one, they came to talk to my uncle, but their questions were the same: 'Did we have to march?' and 'How has Russia come to this?' My uncle spoke very little. He didn't encourage them. He listened and told them to be patient. But they kept coming—and of course the KGB soon knew all about it."

"But how?" Vannie asked. "Doesn't even a general have some privacy?"

"Do you think only foreigners are spied on? Here, the higher up one is, the more closely he's watched. They have so many ways to do it, not just microphones. One evening when I was at my uncle's, they sent a provocateur. He said he was a psychiatrist attached to the Leningrad Army hospital. He claimed he was concerned about the 'mental health' of some of the officers who had been in Czechoslovakia. We both suspected him, the way he plied my uncle with questions and insisted on taking notes. But there was nothing to be done about it."

"But none of the officers—nor your uncle . . . it wasn't a conspiracy. They weren't plotting a revolt."

"My uncle? God, he'd had his fill of revolutions! His father was shot in the Revolution of 1905. His brother was killed in the Civil War. Violence has brought only tragedy to this country. Besides, my uncle was a Communist, a member of the party. He was an officer who always followed orders. He'd swallowed his doubts in the thirties when most of his superiors were shot. Even more during the war—his wife and daughter both died in the siege of Leningrad. After Stalin's death, he hoped for a while we might return to the spirit of 1917. But when they asked him to lead the march into Czechoslovakia, that was too much. He had had enough. A few of us sent petitions, protesting to the Central Committee. He wouldn't sign, but he didn't try to stop us. I remember his words: 'Do it if you must, but expect nobody to defend you. You will pay the price of protest alone.' "

Yuri spoke in a monotone. His legs sprawled on the floor, his head leaning back against the door, he stared up at the sticky cigarette smoke that hung in the corners of the studio.

"When my uncle was in Moscow the last time—it was the middle of December—the deputy chief of the KGB called him in. 'Denounce the traitors who came to see you. By name. In writing.' My uncle refused.

"He was back in Leningrad only two days. I came to have breakfast. I found his body. At first I thought he died in his sleep. I called a doctor, a friend of his who lives nearby. The doctor found a concussion on the back of his skull. We had only talked a few minutes when the KGB arrived. They removed the body and took the doctor and me to headquarters for questioning. They insisted that the doctor was wrong, that my uncle died a natural death. They let me go after a few hours, but told me to say nothing to anyone. I waited. There was no obituary in *Pravda*, no state funeral. I still don't know how or where they buried my uncle. I tried to get hold of the doctor. Couldn't. He was always out or busy. He didn't want to see me. Two weeks later, I was dismissed from the institute, and I came down to Moscow. Nobody here would tell me a thing. Then, ten days ago, they arrested seven of the officers who had come to see my uncle. Last Monday, they searched this studio—that you saw yourself, Vannie. . . . It's only the beginning."

For a few minutes, no one spoke. Drums and brass played the "Rakoczy March." Lydia rose and relit the primus stove to heat the kettle. It was cold in the room.

"And you, Vannie," Yuri asked. "Has the KGB bothered you since last week?"

She nodded. "Could I have a cigarette, Yuri?" He lit two, sprang to his feet and handed her one. "I went up to Leningrad on Saturday," she said. "They followed me the whole time I was there. Today they had an extra militiaman in the courtyard patrolling my entrance. I sneaked out under the fence. I didn't want anybody to know I was coming here."

Yuri sat on the table facing her. "I don't mind if they know you're coming here. I'm not ashamed of you. I'm ashamed of them."

Vannie inhaled her cigarette in short puffs. "I just couldn't stand it. Being watched. Being followed. I . . . I had to get out."

"How do you think we feel? You have been here only two years. We have been born here and can never leave. You have an American passport. You can come and go as you like."

"No, that's not so. Ken can't come back. He called from Rome this morning. His reentry visa has been canceled."

Yuri and Lydia were both startled. They exchanged glances but said nothing. Finally Lydia got up to answer the whistling kettle. She fixed fresh tea. "I'm sorry to hear that, Vannie," she said. "That means you, too, will be leaving. Where will you go? Back to America?"

"London," she said mournfully. "It's our next assignment."

Yuri laughed. "London! Is that a reason to be sad?"

"In a way. I'm leaving you . . . so much behind."

Yuri smiled. "We shall miss you, too, Vannie. But the Soviet Union will manage without you, really it will."

She winced at his irony. Did he think that Russia was merely an amusement for her? Or that she was a meddler?

"How soon do you have to leave?" Lydia asked as she poured more tea.

"In a day or two. As soon as I get permission to take out two paintings." A chorus was singing the finale from *Prince Igor*. "I need . . . advice," Vannie said, pitching her voice under the melody. "I have a third painting. The little Fontanova. You saw it at Rabichov's." She paused. "I haven't declared it."

"Why not?" Yuri asked.

Vannie hesitated. "Because Michael Petrov gave it to me."

"What did you pay for it?" he asked sharply.

"Nothing. It was a gift."

"Impossible. Petrov gives nothing away."

"I'm not sure about that, Yuri. You remember what you said about masks? Well, I think he took his off for a while. We came back from Leningrad together. We had a long talk. I know you don't trust him, but he spoke frankly to me. He feels badly about Czechoslovakia and about your uncle's death too."

Yuri began pacing behind her chair. "Petrov doesn't give a damn about my uncle."

"But it was Petrov who told me the KGB killed him, and that it was the KGB that spread the fake story about an Army plot. Why did he tell me if he didn't want the truth to be known?"

Yuri stared down at her, incredulous. "The truth? That's the last commodity that interests Petrov. He wants to save his own hide. Listen to me, Vannie. Petrov happened to guess wrong last summer, when the Politburo kept changing its mind about Czechoslovakia. Suddenly, when they decided to march, there was Petrov on the losing side. It doesn't happen to him very often. But that's where he is now. Stuck with my uncle, stuck with the truth."

"But he doesn't work for the KGB. . . ."

Yuri shrugged his shoulders. "Who knows? He's put in time with all the special branches. He started out with a taste for good living. Very easy material for the KGB to recruit. He's also done his dirty work for the party's special sector. Now I suppose he's moved over to the GRU—the military intelligence. He probably figures the marshals will take over eventually. But it doesn't make any difference, Vannie. They're all so rotten and twisted, even when they're plotting against each other."

Vannie reflected. "Yuri, why can't you use Petrov? If he's stuck with the truth, why can't he be used to save those officers? To save you?"

Yuri spoke very slowly. "Because the first chance he gets to jump on the winning side, he'll denounce everybody—my uncle, the officers, me. His own babushka."

"That may be, but it might take weeks. In the meantime, you have the same interests. If you could talk with him. . . ."

"It would never work. He's far more skillful at using people than I could ever be. It's his business. And once you start dealing with him, you start thinking like him. And then you become like him. That is a fate I fear more than Siberia."

"Give Petrov back his painting," Lydia advised.

"But why? Nobody besides us knows about it."

Yuri rapped his fingers against the transistor; stretches of staccato interrupted a Gretchaninov lullaby.

"Petrov knows you have it. And he knows you want to keep it. That's enough. Why was there a special militia-man patrolling your entrance today? I'll tell you. Because they suspect you're hiding something they want. Maybe Petrov himself let them know."

"It's just a simple oil painting," Vannie pleaded.

"Nothing, nothing is simple here," Yuri said evenly. "Even a painting can be used as a provocation."

"Then what should I do with it?"

"Leave the painting here in Moscow, Vannie. Go home, now. Straight home. Past the sentry box. Don't go crawling under fences. Just pack your bags and leave."

Vannie rose slowly. Lydia fetched her coat and helped her on with it, brushing away a few remaining flakes of caked-on mud. Vannie held her tears back. "No, *dusha*, don't," Lydia said gently. "There's still too much to do."

Yuri reached for his leather jacket. "Come, Vannie, I'll walk you home."

Yuri walked briskly along the Arbat, his leather jacket open, indifferent to the damp chill. Vannie hurried beside him, trying to keep abreast of his long strides.

In sight of the gingerbread turrets of the Hotel Ukraina, Vannie broke the silence. "I'm only a couple of blocks past the bridge. You should leave me here. This neighborhood is swarming with. . . ."

"I know," he said.

"Please don't be angry with me, Yuri. I've tried to do the right thing . . . to be helpful. It's not easy for a foreigner."

"It's not your fault, Vannie. No one's to blame. It's all built in."

"Perhaps if I knew more . . . or had known whom to talk to when I first came. And this past week . . . I didn't know whom to trust."

He turned to look at her. "Are you wondering whether you trust me?"

"No, Yuri. With you, I just never knew the right questions to ask. Until today. Too late."

He was silent for a moment. "Start to trust again after you have left Russia, Vannie. Not before. This is a country with a cruel history. Some it destroys; some it just wears down. There is no place . . . no patience left for innocents."

A sharp, dry wind blew up just as they reached the compound. They stood facing each other on the avenue.

"Maybe sunshine tomorrow," she said.

"Or snow." He smiled.

"*Do svidanya*, Yuri," she said, extending her hand.

From his jacket pocket, he withdrew a chip of malachite and lay it in her palm. "No more sneaking under fences, Vannie," he said gently.

"Never again," she smiled.

He nodded approvingly. *"Ciao."* His hands thrust into the shallow pockets of his jacket, he turned and strode amiably back toward the bridge.

The telephone rang out in the courtyard as Vannie walked past the sentry box. She glanced disdainfully at the two pairs of observing eyes. "Didn't expect me back so soon, did you?" she said aloud.

The moment of triumph was short-lived. Reaching the second floor, she found her apartment door ajar. The lock had been removed, leaving a round gaping hole. She clenched her teeth. *You won't let up on me, will you?*

She pushed the door open wide. Alla and Ivan were sitting at the kitchen table.

"I'm sorry about the lock, Vannie. The janitor said he'd be back at five to put a new one in." Alla stared at her chipped fingernails as she spoke.

"But why, why?"

"I needed two pictures of you for your exit visa."

"But you have a key! You let yourself in this morning."

Alla shrugged her shoulders. "I must have mislaid it. I couldn't find it. And I needed the photos, or else they wouldn't have your exit visa ready tomorrow."

Here we go again. No lies. Just snatches of the truth.

Ivan beamed as he opened the cardboard box in his lap. "Here it is, gospozha, the best lock in Moscow. And with two keys."

Vannie frowned. "So why don't you install it?"

177

"*Izvinite*, gospozha, but I know nothing about locks."

Vannie held back a cry of rage. "Leave the lock here, Ivan. Go wait in the office until I'm ready. I'll be going to a reception in about an hour."

Vannie waited until she heard him tripping down the stairs. She propped a chair behind the door to keep it closed. "Did he gouge out the lock?"

Alla shook her head. "He asked the janitor to do it. Vannie, don't be angry with him. He has his job to do. Like everyone else." She glanced at her watch. "If you're going to a reception, you'd better get ready. I'll fix your hair if you like."

It was past six by the time Vannie was bathed and dressed. "I don't think the janitor is going to come anymore today, Alla."

"He sometimes works late. I'll stay till he gets here."

"And what if he doesn't show up?"

"There's nothing valuable in the house, is there?"

"No, I suppose not." Vannie had already put her trunk keys and cassette into her black clutch. "But what do I do during the night? Am I supposed to sleep here with the front door open?"

"Keep it barricaded with a couple of chairs. Besides, no stranger is going to wander in. That's what the militiamen are here for."

Vannie suppressed a smile; her private militiaman would undoubtedly protect her apartment from strangers.

Chapter Thirteen

The Swiss residence, a sedate neoclassic town house, was on a residential street halfway between the foreigners' compound and the Kremlin. But Vannie had forgotten the name of the street, and Ivan had forgotten how to get there. He turned and backtracked from the Arbat to the Petrovka three times. "Excuse me, gospozha," he pleaded, "but I'm not a geographer. I'm only a chauffeur."

"The Soviet Union is full of specialists these days," she remarked acidly.

Suddenly spotting several big Western cars parked halfway up the sidewalk, Ivan whizzed between two long lanes of limousines until he reached the militia-guarded entrance of the Swiss residence. Across the street, held back by the policemen, a small crowd of babushkas gathered, holding the hands of their grandchildren. They enjoyed watching the well-dressed foreigners leave their chauffeured cars and pass through the tall iron gates. The guests had been arriving for nearly an hour to pay their respects to the departing Swiss chargé d'affaires.

Bernard Fauvet had come to grief exactly one week earlier—on the Tuesday after Sasha Rabichov's party.

He had just got up from a short nap after lunching alone; his wife Héloïse was in Helsinki on a sauna cure. While he was arranging the place cards for the evening's dinner, the phone rang. A few minutes later, it rang again. And then again. Within a half hour, every Soviet official invited to his dinner had called and canceled. It was his first social setback since his ambassador's recall a year ago had left him acting chief of mission.

Fauvet's ambassador had been a solitary man, who attended but rarely gave diplomatic receptions. In Khrushchev's time, however, he had developed quiet friendships with a few individual Russians. One of them, General Pyotr Zhalkov, came regularly to the residence on his monthly trips from Leningrad. The two men shared an admiration for Napoleon, aged brandy, and a thoughtful game of midnight chess.

Fauvet had hoped to take over this important "contact" after his ambassador's departure, but General Zhalkov had not even answered his invitations. Fauvet decided to find his own path to success. He pondered for several nights how his unique qualities might best serve his country.

He thought himself clever, although not as erudite as his ambassador. He was not bad-looking—small, but lithe, and with a youthful head of brown curly hair. Fauvet assessed his outstanding professional qualities as persistence and *savoir vivre*. They had served him with women as well.

As soon as he moved into the ambassador's residence, he started giving a round of dinner parties. With a meticulous eye for detail, leaving nothing to chance or to Héloïse, he planned the menus, selected the table linens, and ordered a new set of Baccarat crystal from Paris. He gave six dinners the first month, and at each, at least four Soviet officials had been present. "If you throw in the five lunches these past few weeks," he informed his colleagues, "I've already entertained thirty-seven Soviet officials, including three Army colonels. More than my ambassador managed in nearly six years in Moscow!"

Fauvet presided graciously in the silk-paneled dining room, always steering the chitchat to the positive aspects of life in the Soviet Union, convinced that his Russian guests appreciated his tact. Following coffee and Cuban cigars, he would be sure to place a genial arm around the shoulder of at least one Soviet guest—"giving him the feeling that you trust him," he had once explained to Héloïse.

By eleven fifteen the residence was usually empty except for the servants cleaning up and Héloïse devouring the last of the mints. The evening's labors completed, Fauvet would leave the residence and drive to Red Square. Strolling back and forth, sometimes catching the changing of the guard in front of Lenin's tomb, Bernard was often overwhelmed by his success. "Here I am walking beside the Kremlin walls after hosting a gloriously brilliant dinner," he once murmured aloud. When he was certain that Héloïse's swollen face would be buried in her pink satin pillow, he would drive home.

On the Tuesday afternoon following Rabichov's party, Fauvet realized, with a violent flush rushing to his head, that his run of success had been broken. He could not fathom the reasons for Soviet displeasure. His common sense dismissed the possibility that all the Soviet officials—as they claimed—had contracted the grippe that very day and "deeply regretted" being unable to attend the dinner. Since he had already informed his other guests, three ambassadors and four counselors, that important Soviet officials would be present, his immediate task was to avoid well-bred diplomatic snickers. He had to find some Russians—any Russians—quickly.

He had telephoned Vannie Tomkins. "Did you get my invitation for Yuri Zhalkov?"

"Yes, I did, Bernard, but . . ."

"I assume you delivered it."

"I'd rather not discuss it on the phone, Bernard." It was the day after the search at Lydia's, when Fauvet's invitation had been plucked from her hand by the KGB.

"Why not? There is nothing to hide, *chère amie*. His uncle, General Zhalkov, was a frequent guest here. It is all perfectly correct. Will your friend be coming or not?"

"I don't think so, Bernard."

"The invitation was for dinner tonight, Vannie. I did expect a definite answer today. Perhaps you might go back to see him. . . ."

"No. I can't do that, Bernard. Please don't count on him. I'm sorry. I tried."

"Yes, of course. Thank you."

Fauvet put down the phone, which continued to hum long after it was settled in its cradle. He sat down in the oversized chair by the fireplace. What Russian could he

invite at the last minute? At last he recalled the blond
fullness of Ludmilla Rafaelovna, the translator for Interpress, whom he had met at Rabichov's party. Each time
she laughed at his witty remarks, she had thrust her enormous bosom toward him. He phoned Interpress and
addressed her as mademoiselle. Ludmilla Rafaelovna
said she remembered him very well but she would have
to check first. Fifteen minutes later she rang back that
she would be honored to attend his dinner and would he
please call her simply Ludmilla.

That evening Fauvet was particularly pleased with
himself. He chatted in English to Lady Darlington on his
right and then in Russian to Ludmilla, whom he seated
at his left. The food was especially good: crepes with
caviar, *rôti de porc farci*, cheese that had arrived from
Paris, and a superb lemon soufflé that the cook had made.
As a special treat, the white-gloved butlers carried in
several oval-shaped Sheffield bowls overflowing with
black grapes flown down from Helsinki that morning.

He had introduced Ludmilla as a Soviet journalist,
hinting to his diplomatic colleagues that she wielded
considerable influence at *Trud*, the trade-union daily.
Ludmilla knew instinctively to maintain her host's little
masquerade.

The dinner broke up before eleven. "What interesting
Russians one meets here, Bernard," said Lady Darlington as she was helped into her squirrel cape. Bernard
threw Ludmilla a glowing look of gratitude. "Wait at the
corner," he whispered to her. "I'll take you home."

His guests departed, Bernard instructed the butler not

to wait up—he was going for his usual tour of Red Square. He was pleased to inform the servants of his whereabouts; it simplified their reporting for the KGB. *Noblesse oblige.*

At the corner, Fauvet opened the door of his navy-blue Mercedes. Ludmilla darted out of the shadows, and they drove off.

"Ludmilla, you were wonderful. Just perfect," Bernard told her. "I hope I didn't hurt your feelings calling on you so late in the day."

She leaned back on the cream-colored cushions. "Oh, no. I was thrilled." Then she added coyly, "Tell me, Monsieur Fauvet, was I a poor substitute for a very important guest?"

"Now who could be more important than you, Ludmilla?"

She giggled. "Oh, you know. A colonel or a general, maybe."

"A couple of Soviet officials did cancel. An important Kremlin matter at the last minute. But they wouldn't have been half so decorative as you." He patted her knee. "You made an important contribution to tonight's success, Ludmilla."

"I'm so glad, Monsieur Fauvet. And it was the most delicious food I've ever eaten. That pudding for dessert —was it made with Russian lemons?"

"Of course, my dear, Soviet lemons are world-famous. Don't underestimate your country." He squeezed her knee. She giggled again and spread her thighs a little apart.

The boulevard was straight, permitting Bernard to drive with one hand. He slipped the other between her knees. "Yes, Ludmilla, you were a great success tonight. All my guests were impressed." He couldn't get his hand along the inside of her thigh. He pinched the nylon between her knees and took his hand away.

She moved closer to him, stretching her legs out. "You know, Monsieur Fauvet, these stockings are from Paris. A friend gave them to me for Christmas. I love Western things. Sometimes I even get American cigarettes."

Bernard waved a finger at her. "Now, smoking is a bad habit for a woman, Ludmilla. You shouldn't get into our bad Western ways." This time he was able to slip his hand up her thighs until he reached the soft flesh bulging out above her nylon stockings.

"These Western cars are wonderful, don't you think? They warm up so quickly." With that, she slipped off her coat. As she adjusted herself, Bernard's hand climbed higher, into a warm mass of damp hairs.

He took his hand away as he turned the corner into Herzen Street. "Do you live alone, Ludmilla?"

"No, my roommate is home tonight."

Bernard continued along Herzen and then backtracked toward the Lenin Hills. At this hour, no one would be there. He parked the car between two lampposts.

"A little fresh air is good for the digestion, Ludmilla."

They were walking along the road leading down to the river embankment when Ludmilla suddenly danced off into the woods. In the darkness, Bernard heard her chanting, "Ah, the Russian trees. Even at night they are so beautiful. Come, Monsieur Fauvet. Here in the woods, you can really feel the Russian soul."

He started after her, stepping around the bright patches of snow. Before reaching the frolicking Ludmilla, his feet sank into the ground. "Damn it, I'm in the mud," he shouted.

He heard her giggle. "Just a moment, I'll help you out."

As he lifted one foot slowly, the mud oozed out of his shoe, and the other foot sank deeper. He dragged himself to the macadam path. He was furious—his good Belgian shoes ruined chasing an idiotic Russian peasant.

From under the lamppost, he saw Ludmilla emerge from the woods, her coat pulled around her, her evening dress folded neatly in her hand. He put one hand around her shoulders and slipped the other inside the coat. He felt the large, soft breasts still warm and the nipples erect.

"The Moscow night is marvelous, don't you think so, Monsieur Fauvet?" Bernard pressed her closer as they walked up the hill toward the car.

"Yes, I adore the Moscow nights." He tried with one hand to hold both breasts; but they were too large, and he always lost one.

He opened the back door to the car. As she slid in, her coat opened, exposing the ruffle of hair jutting beneath her red girdle. "Do you like my girdle? That comes from America, you know."

She was sprawled across the back seat, and by the light

of the lamppost, he twitted the moist flesh pouting from behind the swollen lips. He climbed in and mounted her astride. His hand reached back and pulled the door shut. She closed her eyes and moaned.

Afterward he looked at her face. She really wasn't very pretty. But her large breasts sprawled beneath his chest were magnificent. He raised himself to look at them again. As he lifted one and squeezed it gently, he saw two faces at the car window, noses pressed against the pane.

Two pairs of eyes, wide open, stared at him. He let Ludmilla's breast drop. The two unshaven men looked at him and grinned. Then they turned and walked into the woods. One of them carried a bottle of vodka, but both were walking steadily. Bernard waited a few minutes without moving.

Ludmilla opened her eyes. "Oh, Bernard, you are marvelous. I love it when you hold them."

He brought his knee over her legs and opened the back door. "Come, get up, Ludmilla. It's time to go home."

Two butlers in white jackets held open the massive iron gates of the Swiss residence as Vannie arrived for Fauvet's farewell party. The broad marble staircase leading from the boiseried entrance foyer sloped gently upward until it reached a carpeted landing, then branched out into the gilded reception room where Prince Yussoupov had once given midnight balls.

Overflowing in a yellow strapless satin gown, Héloïse Fauvet stood framed in the archway of the *petit salon* to receive her guests; her pink, swollen fingers played with a lace handkerchief.

"My husband will be back in a minute, Mrs. Tomkins. He had something very important to discuss with the British ambassador."

"Working to the last minute, your husband." Vannie smiled, touched by Héloïse's baby voice piping out from her enormous cleavage. "I hear he has a very interesting job in Berne."

"Oh, yes, indeed." Héloïse tilted her round face forward—Vannie could smell the chocolates on her breath —and whispered: "The Swiss government is considering the eventual assimilation of the Romansch in the Lower Engadine. Bernard is to be the head of the study program."

"You don't say." Vannie wondered if Héloïse even suspected this pretext for their sudden departure. "But Madame Fauvet," she bantered, "that could be a very dangerous job. They're a tough bunch, those Romansch. They might even start the Swiss Revolution."

Héloïse was flattered. She stood up very tall and smoothed out the creases of her bodice. "Yes, I know. It is a job that requires the highest discretion. Our government has placed great responsibility on my husband's shoulders."

Before she even saw him, Vannie's right hand was plucked and lifted to Bernard Fauvet's avid mouth.

"Dear Vannie, it is really touching that so many close friends have come to say good-bye to us. Isn't it,

Héloïse?" He put his head close to Vannie's. "You know, all the NATO ambassadors have come."

Vannie withdrew herself. "Congratulations, Bernard."

He winked at her knowingly. "I won't keep you. Go say hello. Everybody, just everybody is here tonight."

Vannie crossed the silky Persian rug of the *petit salon* to the main reception hall, brightly lit by half a dozen crystal chandeliers, already crowded with the official diplomatic world of Moscow. Embassy wives munched soggy crumpets. Journalists interviewed each other on the latest political rumors. Ambassadors traded tips on trout fishing. Business representatives reported their eating orgies at Soviet dachas. Selected representatives of the Soviet Foreign Ministry, their unsmiling numbers— were there ten or fifteen tonight?—indicated Russia's esteem for the host country's foreign policy. All the while, nameless Soviet faces brushed past and paused by the little social groups that formed and regrouped.

Vannie slipped a Campari off a passing tray and plunged into the crowd. Handshakes, smiles, greetings. "Did you have a good time in Leningrad?" "If spring doesn't come, I'm going to commit suicide." "I found tomatoes on the market today." "I saw this Russian just blowing his nose—without even a handkerchief!"

Vannie suddenly looked up. There was someone watching her—not a nameless face but a smiling woman. The gray eyes found their object, and she was no more than six feet away. Vannie watched Simone Durand move toward her.

"I'm so glad to see you again, Mrs. Tomkins."

"How interesting to see you, Madame Durand. You stayed here longer than you expected."

"It is terribly hard for me to leave this city. I have so many friends here, you know."

"Like Sasha Rabichov? Have you seen him lately?"

Simone Durand showed her pearly teeth. "Why, yes. He left for Paris this morning. I went to the airport to see him off. As a matter of fact, we spoke about you. He was wondering if you had seen your pictures."

"My what?"

"Why, my dear, there was a photographer at Sasha's exhibition. Didn't you notice? There was a very bad picture of me, but several fine ones of you. Talking to your friends, of course. Oh, Mrs. Tomkins, have I surprised you? I'm so sorry. You must be terribly upset since you walked in on that search."

"I was upset for my friends, Madame Durand. I'm very fond of them."

"Of whom? Little Lydia? Oh, my dear, don't you realize that she set it all up for you?"

"That is quite impossible, Madame Durand. I have always visited her on Tuesdays and Fridays. It was the first and only time I came on a Monday. I was not expected."

"But, Mrs. Tomkins, everyone knows that little Lydia reports to the KGB."

"Doesn't everyone these days, Madame Durand?" Vannie tried to paste a smile on her face to match Simone's.

"You shouldn't be so cynical, my dear. There are wonderful people you can meet in this country. You musn't be mistrustful. But you don't have much time left, do you?"

"No, I intend to leave as soon as I get permission to take my paintings out."

"That isn't always easy, Mrs. Tomkins. Do you think you will get permission to take out the Fontanova?"

"How. . . . I. . . ." The words wouldn't come out. *God damn Petrov. Has he already switched sides? How else would she know if he hadn't told her?* Vannie shivered in her sleeveless chestnut silk.

Simone watched her. "You're cold, my dear. A cocktail party is not a place to discuss paintings, it it? Perhaps we could meet tomorrow. Have you been to the Turkish baths yet?"

Vannie shook her head.

Simone smiled benignly. "You really should come. I'll meet you there. We can take one together. It's an unforgettable experience."

"I've already had quite enough unforgettable experiences, thank you."

"But, my dear, we should meet and have a long talk before you leave Moscow. Perhaps if you don't get permission to take out the Fontanova, you might want to leave it with me. I have good friends here who would keep it for you."

Vannie's breath was short. "Madame Durand, I won't even ask how you know I have the Fontanova. But tell me . . . please . . . why do you want it?"

Simone put a thick hand on Vannie's bare shoulder.

"I don't want it for myself, my dear. I simply want to help you. You are so young, and you do not really know this country." She shook her head sadly. "You will never get that painting out by yourself."

"You seem to be very sure of that."

"Oh, my dear . . . may I call you Vannie? There is such a difference in our ages." She wrinkled her nose, but her light gray eyes didn't change color. "I'm not sure of anything. But I too was once young . . . and careless."

"What is that supposed to mean?"

Simone's eyes narrowed. "That you shouldn't have left your red address book on the night train to Leningrad."

"Oh, no . . . no. . . ." Vannie closed her eyes; a thousand images tumbled from all sides . . . cameras, hidden lights. She opened them again. Simone Durand had not moved.

"Don't worry, my dear. I really want to be of help. Your address book is perfectly safe in my possession. I shall be happy to return it. Tonight. Let's say at nine thirty in front of Tchaikovsky Hall. Outside, toward the corner of Gorki Street. And do bring the Fontanova with you. We shall make a friendly trade." She pressed Vannie's limp hand. Then she was gone.

Vannie felt the wet glass of her forgotten Campari. Without moving, she reached for the tray of a passing waiter. The glass missed. It fell on the patterned carpet, breaking quietly at her feet.

"One too many, old girl?" Hardy Summers bent down

and wrapped the larger pieces of glass in his handkerchief.

"I'm sorry, Hardy. I was sure the tray was there."

"Don't apologize to me, my love. It's not my establishment.'"

"But the tray was there," Vannie insisted. "The waiter must have moved it."

"That's what he gets paid to do."

"You don't understand, Hardy. Nothing is where it's supposed to be."

"Neither are you, Vannie. You should be home packing, instead of talking to steely-eyed old biddies."

"Yes, that's where I want to go. Home. I can't find my bearings anymore."

"It's a big world, Moscow, once you get to know it."

"It's not that it's big, Hardy. It's another world, a world of . . . now-you-see-it, now-you-don't." She paused. "Tell me truthfully. Am I losing my mind?"

He put his arm under her elbow and steered her toward the door. "Not that I've noticed—yet. But I'll lose my patience if you hang around Moscow anymore. Try and take the plane out tomorrow, will you?"

Vannie nodded.

The Fauvets were busy greeting late arrivals. She slipped past them down the marble staircase.

The door to the apartment was still ajar, the foyer light on. "Are you still here, Alla?" Vannie called. There was no answer.

She pulled the chair from beside the foyer table and propped it against the door. She went into the bedroom, switched on the light, checked under the bed and in the clothes closets. There was no one there. She switched the light off. Back through the living room into the kitchen; the sudden light sent three large roaches running for cover. There was no one in the apartment.

Fearing someone might enter unheard, she fetched four wineglasses and placed them on the chair against the door. She turned off the remaining lights, then opened the door to the storage closet. The light inside was on. Who had forgotten to turn it off? Unimportant, she decided; the trunk was locked. She took the key out of her evening bag, opened the trunk and disentangled the Fontanova from her ski clothes. Still in her coat, she carried the canvas through the darkened apartment into the living room.

There were no blinds or shutters. The spotlights illuminating the compound cast a vague light through the closed draperies. Vannie sat down on a hardbacked chair by the dining-room table. In the semidarkness, she clutched her painting with one hand and her evening bag in the other.

What does Simone Durand want from me? Why does she want this painting? Vannie's fingers felt along the wooden rectangular backing of the canvas. *There's nothing, nothing here. No microfilm. No secret message. I have nothing for her.*

She put her bag down on the table. She tapped the rich

texture of the Fontanova's brush strokes as if a secret might ooze out. The oil held firm. *But she thinks I have something. What?*

My address book—how did she know about it? I told no one—well, just Alla. But Simone Durand said she had the book in her possession. Vannie clenched her teeth and squeezed her eyes shut. *I didn't leave it on the train. Nothing happened on that train. But even if someone found it . . . if he found it . . . he wouldn't, he couldn't have given it to her!*

Was it worth it, the trip to Leningrad? A birthday party for Andrey—someone you'll never see again? To have lost your address book in exchange for forty minutes of Russian folk songs to play on an evening of nostalgia?

Perhaps to prove to herself that it was worth it or simply to make the moment more bearable, she went into the bedroom and brought the tape recorder to the dining-room table. Still in the half-darkness, she took the cassette out of her evening bag and slipped it into the recorder. She pushed the button down to Play.

There were voices. Russians. Two men. No, three. And then Vannie heard the name of Zhalkov. Once and then a second time. Abruptly, she switched off the tape.

She went into the kitchen and turned on both water faucets till they splashed loudly against the steel sink. She pushed the rewind button until the tape was back at the beginning. Then, lowering the volume, she held the tape recorder against her ear and let it play.

The first sounds were three sharp raps on a door. Then the squeak of its opening and the shuffle of footsteps. Then the door slammed shut.

A voice: "Comrade General, you are requested to come with us immediately."

A second voice, older and deeper: "How dare you wake me at this hour!"

"Our colonel works only at night, Comrade Zhalkov. The colonel regrets the inconvenience."

"If your colonel wants to talk to me, he can ask my adjutant for an appointment. Now get out!"

Suddenly, a third voice, young and impatient: "You don't understand, Zhalkov. This is not an invitation. You have no choice. Get dressed."

The first voice again, mocking now. "And not in your uniform, Comrade General. We want you in civilian clothes."

"So . . . so . . ."—the older man, breathing heavily —"so this is how your Lyonka Brezhnev is doing it, like in the old days. Go back and tell your colonel that Stalin is dead. The KGB can no longer summon generals in the middle of the night."

"Tell him yourself, Zhalkov," the young man's voice snapped. "We all leave together."

The old man was now panting audibly: "Then I will put on my uniform, with decorations. We will take my car, with my driver. . . ."

Four swift footsteps.

"Stay where you are, Zhalkov," the first voice shouted. "Don't touch that telephone again. Mitya, help him

dress. And, General, better take your winter coat and fur-
lined boots. You'll need them."

"You scum!" the old man gasped. "You'll be in Siberia
before me."

The sounds of scuffling. Shattered glass. Objects fall-
ing. Then another fall, a heavy flat thud. A deep groan.
Silence.

Finally the young voice, frightened: "Maybe . . .
maybe he's faking."

Two footsteps. Silence again.

"Mitya, you clumsy fool—why did you hit him?"

"He would have been out the door if I hadn't. . . .
What will we tell the colonel?"

"You'd better think of something, Mitya, it was you
who did it. All right, let's get him on the bed now. Careful . . . that's it . . . fix the covers now . . . good. Just
right."

"What shall we do with the lamp?"

"Put the pieces in your pocket, we'll get rid of them
later. Straighten out that chair. Good. Let's go."

Then there was silence.

Vannie stopped the recorder and stood in the middle
of the kitchen, stunned. Michael Petrov had taped the
recording of General Zhalkov's murder on the other
track of Andrey's cassette!

Chapter Fourteen

Vannie took the cassette out of the tape recorder. With her fingernail, she nicked the identification slot on the Zhalkov side, leaving Andrey's songs on the other track unmarked. She went into the living room and slipped the cassette back into her evening bag.

Simone Durand knows only that Michael Petrov gave me something—something to do with General Zhalkov's death. She suspects that I have proof that it was the KGB and not the Leningrad captain who killed him. That bitch: She was the one who slipped the onionskin paper into my shopping bag in Sasha Rabichov's kitchen.

"Cool, cool," Vannie told herself. She sat down on the couch and pulled out another cigarette. She couldn't find a match. She licked the filter tip with her tongue.

But Simone Durand doesn't know the proof is on the cassette. She thinks it has something to do with the Fontanova. With her twisted mind, she's probably convinced there's a message in invisible ink on the canvas. Or a microfilm slotted into the wooden frame. Is that why Michael Petrov gave me the Fontanova—and then told her about it—as a decoy?

She looked at her watch. She had about an hour before

meeting Simone. *If I give her the Fontanova, she'll never
give it back. By tomorrow morning she'll know there are
no secrets in it. Then they'll search me at the airport—
and find the cassette.*

*Vannie Tomkins, stop playing dangerous games with
professionals. Just give her the cassette and say, "Here is
what you're really looking for. Take it. I want no part of
you, KGB, GRU, or whatever you are. I just want my
paintings and my address book. You fight your own bat-
tles and stop using me!"*

But Vannie knew it was too late for that. Had the orig-
inal KGB story not been planted in her bag; had Ken
not passed the phony story on to the London newspaper;
had she not gone to Lydia's the day of the search; had she
waited for Nancy to share her compartment for Leningrad . . . and not left her address book on the train with
Alexander Starr; had she not gone with Michael Petrov
to his dacha, then, perhaps, there would be an easy way
out. But she couldn't see one anymore. There were no
more straight roads—only blind curves leading down
and under.

She got up and went into the dark kitchen, felt for the
matchbox beside the stove, and lit her cigarette. The
blue flame chased the roaches into hiding. She flinched at
the remembered words: "You and your husband have
whitewashed a murder." Petrov might jump off the losing side, but Vannie would not. There were too many
innocent people at stake: Yuri Zhalkov, the young officers in Leningrad. And there was her own sense of

honor. At all costs, she was determined to protect the Zhalkov cassette.

Then she smiled to herself. *Simone Durand thinks I'm a silly naïve fool. If she continues to think so, I may yet keep my Fontanova and get back my address book, too.*

Vannie crushed out the cigarette and opened the utility drawer, gingerly feeling the tools in the darkness. Her hands found a pair of pliers and a small knife with a thin blade. She brought them into the living room.

Using one tool and then the other, she detached the linen canvas from the frame of the Fontanova. She brought the wooden rectangle into the storeroom and locked it into the trunk.

She rolled the linen canvas, painted side out so that it wouldn't crack, and stuffed the hollow center with old copies of *Pravda*. Then she put it into her shopping bag —the same one into which Simone had slipped her phony story about the Zhalkov assassination. *Poetic justice*, Vannie mused.

She left the pliers, knife, and nails on the table, just in case "someone" dropped in while she was gone. She checked her handbag; she had both her trunk keys and the cassette. She was ready.

The phone in the militia box rang as she strode across the courtyard. "That's right, comrades. I've left. The door's open. Go in and look." She swung her purse in one hand and her shopping bag in the other. When she reached the avenue, a taxi pulled up to the curb. She hesitated a moment, then chose to walk.

She reached Tchaikovsky Hall as the doors opened for intermission. The concert crowd started to trickle down the front steps. A few crossed over to Mayakovsky Square, gathering under the white globes hanging from branched iron lampposts. Vannie glanced at the billboard: An Evening of Shostakovich, David Oistrakh Conducting. She took tentative steps toward Gorki Street. Perhaps Simone Durand was already waiting at the corner. No—she had said in front of the concert hall. Then Vannie felt a heavy hand on her sleeve.

"I'm here, my dear. How nice of you to come."

"How very nice of you, Madame Durand. I hope I'm not inconveniencing you."

Simone said nothing. She searched Vannie's face. "I have an extra ticket for the concert. It's very good. Why don't you come back in with me and we can talk afterwards?" The woman's face had not changed: the bright gray eyes, the suspended smile.

"I think it would get me home too late. I might be leaving Moscow tomorrow, you know."

"Of course, my dear. It was inconsiderate of me to forget. Wait here just a moment. I'll tell my friends that I'm not coming back for the second half."

She went back in the lobby and disappeared behind the inner doors. A few minutes later she returned with her coat on her arm, and they started toward Gorki Street.

"There's an unpretentious restaurant in the Hotel Sofia," Simone suggested. "Shall we try it?"

It was not yet ten o'clock, but the broad avenue was

nearly empty. The Hotel Sofia faced on Gorki, but Simone steered Vannie down a side street. "The restaurant has a separate entrance," she explained.

The vestibule was lit garishly by an overhead chain of multicolored bulbs. They checked their coats and climbed a flight of concrete stairs. The restaurant itself was on street level; its windows looked out on Gorki.

All the tables were taken, mostly by Russian and Bulgarian men in their shirt sleeves. A lone waiter shuffled through the airless room. Thick smoke hovered over littered tables of greasy dishes and empty wine bottles. Swarthy heads—several sporting embroidered hats from the provinces—bent over glasses of vodka and rakhia.

Two Armenians rose from a window table. Simone gestured to Vannie. "Shall we sit there and wait till it's cleaned up? It's rather cozy in that alcove."

Without waiting for an answer, she led the way. They sat opposite each other. Vannie dropped her shopping bag onto the chair between them. The waiter cleared the table of half-empty glasses and butt-filled ashtrays, uncovering blotches of spilled red wine.

Simone brushed away the menu. "Two orders of stuffed grape leaves, please, and a bottle of red Gamza." She smiled at Vannie. "That is all right with you, isn't it? Bulgarian wine is quite good if it isn't taken seriously." Vannie nodded. She hadn't eaten since her lunch at the window ledge, watching her militiaman.

"It was a terribly exciting concert, Vannie. I'm sorry for your sake that you couldn't at least hear the second half."

"You would make a wonderful cultural guide, Madame Durand."

"You're flattering me, Vannie, but I do love music. Shostakovich is an old friend of mine. But you foreigners always seem to be more interested in meeting writers or painters than composers."

"Would you excuse me for a moment? I have to go to the ladies' room." In her haste, Vannie missed the second step down from the alcove. As her hand leaped forward to grasp the nearest table, her purse knocked over a plate of greasy lamb bones. She murmured apologies to a glazed-eyed Georgian and headed for the cloakroom stairs.

Something's wrong, she thought. *I don't like this restaurant and I hate stuffed grape leaves.* She inserted two coppers in the coin slot and dialed.

"Nancy? Vannie. Please pick me up at the Hotel Sofia in about fifteen minutes."

"I can't, Vannie. I have company. Why don't you take a taxi?"

"Nancy, please, it's important."

"All right. Fifteen or twenty minutes."

When Vannie returned, the food was already on the table, the bottle of Gamza leaning against the rim of an ice-filled wine chiller.

"Forgive me for starting, Vannie, but I was famished. I never seem to get a chance to eat when I'm in Moscow. Too excited seeing friends, I suppose. Do try the grape leaves. They're better here than in Bulgaria. Perhaps we should order some ayvar salad? It's a Balkan specialty and quite delicious."

"I'm not really very hungry."

"You'll never be able to leave tomorrow on an empty stomach, now will you?" Vannie started to pick apart the slimy green rolls.

"And the wine is worth tasting. It does have a certain quality." Vannie shook her head and covered the glass with her hand. *Who are those three men at the next table?* she wondered. There had only been a young couple there when they had entered.

Then she saw her shopping bag hanging on the back of Simone's chair. The older woman followed her gaze. "Why did you take the Fontanova off the frame, Vannie?"

Vannie had her answer ready. "It seemed easier to carry it that way. I walked here, you know."

Simone was not content. "I wanted the painting exactly as you received it. It's a pity you took it off the frame."

"Well, if it's the frame you really want, I'll take home the canvas and send you the frame in the morning."

Simone raised her wineglass to her lips. She savored the Gamza slowly, swishing it from one side of her mouth to the other. Finally she swallowed and put down her glass. "I'll think about it, Vannie. Let's finish dinner first, shall we?"

Vannie ate another stuffed grape leaf. It had a wretched taste. Balkan turds. But she didn't want to offend Simone. Not right now. "You do have my address book with you?" she asked.

Simone smiled, a wide, warm pearly grin. "I'm so sorry, my dear. I didn't bring it with me. I didn't know when I left home that the two of us would be having dinner tonight."

"Why didn't you go back for it after Fauvet's reception?"

"I truly intended to. But it was such a rush I barely made the concert in time." She took Vannie's hand in both of hers. "But if you like, why don't you come back home with me and get it?"

Vannie felt a cramp in her abdomen. She snatched her hand back from Simone. "How do I know you even have it?"

"How, then, would I know about it?"

"My husband's secretary may have told you." Vannie loosened her belt a notch.

"My, my, my, how distrustful we are! I've never even met your husband's secretary. But you're not feeling well, are you? Here, have a sip from my glass. It might make you feel better."

Vannie shook her head. The pain was coming in waves. She clutched her purse. "I have to go to the toilet."

"But, my dear, you just went there. Is it too warm here for you?"

Vannie covered her mouth with the white linen napkin.

"You should have told me that grape leaves don't

agree with you. We would have ordered something else."

She got up and came around the table. She lay her hand on Vannie's shoulder. "You poor thing. Just wait here, my dear, and I'll bring up our things. You'll feel better in the fresh air. And then I'll take you home."

She walked toward the door that led down to the cloakroom.

Vannie pushed her chair from the table and got up.

The pain was weaving around her belly and heaving upward. She clutched the napkin back to her mouth. Holding onto the edge of the table with one hand, she let herself down the two steps. The door to the hotel lobby was at the other end. A thin, sharp cramp doubled her over. She muffled the moan in her napkin.

Her legs rigid, she shuffled her way along the narrow aisle. "I can't throw up here." She leaned on the back of someone's chair. He didn't turn around. Nobody rose to help. *Everyone thinks I'm drunk.*

A new thick pain hit her in the middle. She pressed the napkin closer against her mouth and threw her head back. Then she leaned her whole body against the swinging door.

She bumped into a bearded Bulgarian. "Excuse me . . . I'm not feeling well. . . . The street, *pozhaluista, Gorkova ulitsa.*" He held her by the elbow and guided her through the lobby. Then she felt a fresh breeze. She was cold. And there was another hand under her other arm. Someone pushed her into a car.

"No," she screamed. She leaned over before anyone

could shut the door and vomited beside the curb. An arm pulled her back, and the car started.

"Oh, don't drive, please. I feel so sick. Open the window," she wailed.

"The window is open, Vannie. You'll be home in a few minutes." Nancy sped down the Petrovka.

Chapter Fifteen

The door to the living room was open, the sunlight filtering brightly through the yellow draperies. Nancy was sitting beside her in the darkened bedroom when Vannie opened her eyes. She was still wearing the chestnut silk dress she had put on for Fauvet's reception. Alla moved out of the shadows toward the window.

"No, please. Leave the curtains closed."

Nancy leaned forward. "Would you like some water, Vannie?"

"No, no water. I don't want anything." She sat up, resting her back against the headboard. "I'm still dressed." And then it all came back. "My purse? Where's my purse?"

"Right by your elbow," Nancy said quietly. Vannie clutched at it, funbled with the opening: keys, cassette. . . . "Is this all I had with me? No shopping bag?"

"No coat either," Nancy said. "Did you lose it? Want me to call the restaurant?"

"Fat chance." Vannie bit her lip. Leaning on her hands, she managed to swing her legs off the bed. "My paintings, Alla. Please call now."

209

"I did, Vannie." Alla paused. "The Ministry of Culture said no."

"What reason did they give?"

"None. Vannie, I'm sorry. People in this country do things sometimes . . . for no reason." Alla looked away.

Vannie nodded. She felt warm tears in her eyes. *No, if I cry now, I'm finished.* "Alla, please get my visa. And a ticket. I've got to make the Alitalia plane. Today."

Wordlessly, Alla left the room. Nancy closed the door. "Now suppose you tell me what happened last night. Another Russian friend celebrating his birthday?"

Vannie shook her head, then pressed her temples to subdue the rattle. "I really don't know myself what happened."

Nancy rose. "I can't understand you, Vannie. Hardy Summers told you, I told you: Stay home. Yet you keep going back like a moth to the flame. Why?"

"Ask the moth."

"I'm asking *you*."

Vannie stood up. "Don't be angry, Nancy. I'm very grateful to you for last night."

"Then try at least to stay out of trouble till you leave for the airport." Nancy threw her coat around her shoulders. "I'm late for work."

Vannie followed her into the foyer. "Just one last favor, Nancy, please. Stop by the janitor's office, across from the militia box. Ask him to come over now and bring a small saw. Here, give him five rubles."

"I thought Russians don't care about money."

"He's a Georgian." Nancy took the five-ruble note and left. The front door remained ajar.

Vannie went into the storage closet and pulled down an empty canvas suitcase. Then she unlocked the trunk and lifted out the wooden frame she had detached from the Fontanova. She carried both the picture frame and the suitcase into the foyer.

The compound's chief janitor stood in the open doorway, his potbelly dripping over a low-slung plastic belt. He looked at her suspiciously with one eye. The other was glass.

"I have this old frame here. And I need something to stiffen the sides of this suitcase. Can you saw the frame in four pieces for me?"

He nodded. Withdrawing a string from the pocket of his faded blue-denim jacket, he measured the suitcase and then the frame. "It won't be long enough," he said.

"That's all right. The wood doesn't have to go completely around."

"I have some longer pieces in the shed."

"No," said Vannie sharply. "I want this wood."

She watched him bring the frame into the kitchen and lay it on the table. In measured, sullen movements, he sliced the frame into four slats.

"Is that all?" he asked.

"No. I'd like you to install the front-door lock. You were supposed to do it yesterday. Remember?"

He examined the lock, then walked to the door and, with a penknife, started scraping to enlarge the hole.

Vannie threw the four slats of the picture frame into her suitcase and brought it to the bedroom.

The phone rang. It was Alla. "They won't give me your visa, Vannie. They want a clearance from customs first."

"But I have nothing to clear. I thought you would pack the trunk after I leave."

"They don't want to see the trunk. They want to see you."

Vannie looked at her watch. It would be a race if she were ever to make the Alitalia flight. "Send the car back for me. I'll meet you at customs in half an hour."

It took her fifteen minutes to pack the suitcase, stuffing the corners with underwear. Then she carefully laid the four slats of wood lengthwise along each side. As she zipped her suitcase closed, she felt the single eye behind her. She turned.

"The lock is in," the janitor said, staring at her suitcase.

"That was quick." She foraged in her bag for another five rubles. He pocketed the bill and left. As she had expected, he had left only one key on the kitchen table.

It would take about an hour before the janitor's report reached the authorities. She had an hour to get back to the apartment before they did. As an added precaution, she locked her suitcase inside the trunk.

She quickly brushed her teeth, changed into a black wool suit, and smoothed down her hair. Then, her leather handbag slung over her shoulder, an abstract

painting under each arm, she trudged down to the courtyard.

Ivan Fyodorovich was dancing around the car with a
scrubbing brush.

"Not now, Ivan. I'm in a hurry."

"Just two more minutes, gospozha." When he finished
drying the windshield, he tucked his brushes and cloths
under the driver's seat and slid the paintings in beside
him. "To the customs?" he asked.

"No, Ivan. To the Tretyakov."

It was only a five-minute drive to the museum's side
entrance where Vannie had brought her paintings for in-
spection the day before. "Wait here, Ivan, I won't be
long." She lifted out the two canvases herself.

The gray-haired curator in the "judgment room,"
wearing the same musty dress, was giggling into the telephone. She put a hand over the mouthpiece when she
saw Vannie.

"I told you yesterday, Gospozha Tomkins . . ." she said
sternly.

Vannie interrupted. "I know the Tretyakov doesn't
consider them national treasures. But since you have so
little modern Russian painting, I've decided to donate
them to the museum."

The curator abruptly put down the receiver. "We do
not hang abstract paintings in the Tretyakov."

"Perhaps someday you will." Vannie propped the
paintings on the marble mantelpiece.

The curator sprang to her feet. "Gospozha Tomkins,
we cannot accept. . . ."

"Then don't. I'm leaving them here anyway." Vannie was already across the room.

"But we are not. . . ." Vannie heard no more as she slammed the door and dashed down the steps.

The Impala was no longer parked at the entrance. She ran to the corner; it wasn't in front of the museum either. Then she heard Ivan's mincing feet behind her. "The car is back here, gospozha," he announced breathlessly.

"But you were already parked. Why did you drive away?"

"I had to get gas."

"You went for gas yesterday."

"There was no gas at the station yesterday."

"Why didn't you go to another station?"

"There's only one station here with Super."

"Only one in all Moscow?" Vannie exclaimed. "And you call this a city? It's a village."

"Gospozha, it's not a village. It's not a city." He spread his hands in total confusion. "It's Moscow."

Ivan circled around Komsomol Square, passing the Leningrad Station twice before finding the entrance to the customs depot. He followed an open truck into the rambling complex of two- and three-story gray stone buildings, then maneuvered in and out of a series of loading depots. At last Vannie spotted a hand-lettered sign: Administration.

Alla was waiting in the vestibule. "You're late," she said dully. Vannie followed her down the hall into a cluttered office, with dusty mimeographed forms heaped over half-open file cabinets. A swarthy Uzbek girl in a white organdy blouse received them. "Comrade Andronov will be here in half an hour. He is coming specially for you."

"I can't wait that long," Vannie snapped. "I have to make a plane today."

Alla tugged at Vannie's sleeve. "Don't fight. It's no use." Vannie sat down on a round wooden stool beside the door. She pulled out a cigarette. The first puff shot down her chest into her raw stomach. She crushed it out with her heel and threw the dead butt into an over-stuffed waste can. Alla leaned against the wall with her eyes closed. *That's the way to do it*, Vannie mused. *Shut your eyes and cop out.*

Why this concerted effort to stall me? Does everyone suspect I'm hiding something? What's his name— Andropov? Whom does he work for? Customs and who else? Did Simone Durand tell him about the Fontanova —that I detached the canvas from the frame? If he keeps me waiting much longer, the KGB will get to the apartment before I'm back.

As Vannie lit another cigarette, the Uzbek girl said: "Comrade Andronov will see you now. Second door to the left."

The room was bare, with chipped paint peeling off the pale-green walls. Two strips of mangy brown cloth partly curtained the single window. Comrade Andronov, a massive figure, sat behind a pine desk with ringed fingers clasped in front of him. A large, white-maned head, a gold stickpin piercing his red silk tie—no, Vannie decided, this was no lowly customs inspector, and this bare room could hardly be his main office.

Andronov rose easily despite his bulk and strolled to the window, staring out at the loading ramp. "Please, Mrs. Tomkins, do take a seat." The narrow-planked floor squeaked as she pulled up a metal folding chair to face him.

"I have only a few routine questions." He turned around. "Where are your paintings?" he asked.

Vannie looked up at him, holding his gaze. "What difference does it make? I haven't received permission to take them out, so . . . I'm leaving them here in Moscow."

"Where exactly?"

"They're already at the Tretyakov Gallery."

"I see." He stood pensively at the window and then returned slowly to his desk. "All three paintings?" he asked.

Vannie held her breath. "Yes, all three are in Moscow."

He opened the top drawer and pulled out a sheet of lined paper. "Suppose you write down their exact location."

"I can't write Russian."

"In English, then." He handed her his fountain pen and watched her intently as she wrote:

"One oil, Kondrashev; one oil Ulyanov: Tretyakov Gallery. One oil, Fontanova: care of Simone Durand, address unknown."

"That will do very nicely," he said, folding the paper and slipping it into his breast pocket.

He opened his gold cigarette case. "Would you like one?" He lit it for her with his customary flourish of the match. "I'm afraid there is no ashtray," he apologized. "We are forced to use the floor."

He's keeping me here, purposely. I'll miss my plane!

"May I express my regrets, Mrs. Tomkins, that you are unable to take your paintings with you? But I trust you have some other pleasant reminder of your stay here in the Soviet Union."

"I've picked up three Russian dolls and a dozen Easter eggs. Thank you."

"And music? Surely you still have the cassette of your friend's songs. The one in Leningrad. Andrey . . . ? I forget his patronymic for the moment. You will take it with you when you leave? I'm sure your husband will enjoy hearing it."

Vannie trembled as cigarette ash dropped on her lap. "Perhaps. I don't know," she stammered.

He thrust his bulky, ringed fingers across the desk. "*Bon voyage*, Mrs. Tomkins. Your visa will be ready at one o'clock." Vannie shook his hand, shuddering at his smile of even gold teeth, and then walked out to the loading ramp.

Alone in the borrowed office, Konstantin Andronov watched through the window until he saw Vannie and Alla drive off in the black Impala. Then he picked up the phone to call Petrov.

217

Chapter Sixteen

The front door to the apartment was double-locked when Vannie returned; she had only closed it when she had left. The light was now on in the storage room, too. But there was no sign that they had touched the trunk; the suitcase was still inside.

Vannie had little time to reflect on whether the KGB had come to search the aprtment thoroughly or merely to frighten her. It was nearly one o'clock. Her plane left at three.

By one thirty, Vannie's suitcase was already in the car. Too impatient to sit while the motor idled, she paced in the courtyard until Alla arrived with her visa and ticket.

Alla declined to accompany her to the airport. "I get weepy at the last minute. Better here." It was a Russian embrace—a bear hug with a kiss on both cheeks. Vannie waved to her from the rear window as Ivan maneuvered the large black sedan around the narrow roadway. Sinking deeply against the back cushions, Vannie nodded to the two pairs of militia eyes following the car's exit. "Write it down," she said aloud. "Vannie Tomkins. Left, one forty. Forever. I hope you miss me."

It was a few minutes past two when Ivan pulled up to

the entrance of Sheremetyevo Airport. Nancy and Hardy Summer were waiting for her at the curbside. Hardy opened the car door and pulled out Vannie's suitcase. "They've got three of them waiting for you at the check-in counter," he said.

Nancy glanced impatiently at her watch. "I'm not too late," Vannie assured her. "With luck, you'll be rid of me in forty-five minutes."

The clatter of their footsteps on the black marble floor echoed curiously in the vast silence of the airport's main hall. Only two planes were scheduled for departure: Alitalia for Rome and Aeroflot for Peking. Vannie heard her named called. Laura and Federico Succioli, descending the visitors' staircase, crossed the hall swiftly to greet her.

"Five minutes, Nancy," she pleaded. "I'll join you at the check-in counter." Nancy nodded and followed Hardy on to passport control.

Vannie hugged the Succiolis fiercely. "I'm so glad to see you here. I feel like so much cargo ready to be shipped out."

"Mario Campini said the same thing two days ago," Federico said.

"But how did you know I was taking the Alitalia today?"

Laura was chagrined. "We didn't, Vannie. Mario's wife and children are going out on the same plane. We brought them to the airport."

"But you are leaving so suddenly," the ambassador said. "Another unscheduled departure?"

Vannie nodded. "Ken's been refused a return visa. He wanted me out quickly. And at this point I'm more than ready to leave. Maybe someday I'll discover why."

"You mean why Ken was refused a return visa?"

Vannie shook her head. "No, I'll find that out soon enough. But why do we all have to sneak away like this —Mario, the Fieldses, Fauvet?"

"Among others," the ambassador remarked dryly.

"But why, Federico? Because of the Zhalkov case? None of us even knew the general—"

"That's unimportant," the ambassador interrupted. "You didn't have to know him. Just knowing *about* him was too much. Besides, Vannie, we're always suspect here, no matter what we do, simply because of what we are. That's why they control us so thoroughly."

"But all those people spying on us, installing microphones, tapping telephones, searching apartments—and this country can't even produce a decent tea kettle! Can't they put those people to better use?"

"That's what holds it all together." The ambassador smiled indulgently. "Tell me, Vannie, have you been able to take anything with you?" She looked at him, startled. "Your paintings, I mean," he added.

"No," said Vannie evenly. "Nothing."

"Is that why you're so upset?" Laura asked.

"No. . . . Well, yes, partly. . . . I don't know. It's strange. Ten days ago, I thought I'd got to know this country so well in such a short time. Now it seems I've got such a long way to go just to get on that plane."

Laura smiled. "Forgive us, Vannie, but we cannot stay

until your plane leaves." She leaned forward to kiss Vannie's cheek.

"But I'll be seeing you both again soon, won't I? In Rome or in London?"

Federico's eyes clouded over. "*Sì, cara.* Sooner than you suspect. *Arrivederci.*"

As Vannie waved a last good-bye, Ivan Fyodorovich rushed in breathlessly. "*Do svidanya, gospozha.* Say good-bye, please, to Gospodin Tomkins. Tell him I wish him everything good." Vannie smiled and shook his hand.

Three plainclothesmen in dark suits were loitering in a far corner as Vannie arrived to check in. Each had a boarding card prominently displayed in his breast pocket.

"Here, Vannie," Hardy called. He was straddling her suitcase in front of the Alitalia counter.

A Soviet Aeroflot girl took Vannie's passport and ticket, as Hardy lifted the suitcase onto the luggage scale. While the blond Aeroflot girl studied her ticket, Vannie filled out her currency declaration. "Are those three goons going to fly out with me?" Vannie whispered to Hardy.

"No. They'll stay with you just as far as the tarmac. You're not smuggling out icons, I hope."

The Aeroflot girl made out a baggage ticket and a boarding card. Vannie extended a hand to receive them. But the girl gave the documents to a green-uniformed KGB border guard at the adjacent customs counter.

The young guard opened the passport and studied the

photograph, looking up twice to match it against her face. Satisfied, he put the passport aside.

"Is this the only luggage you have?"

"Yes."

He lifted it from the scale and lay it on a table behind him. "Please open it," he ordered.

Vannie stepped on the scale and jumped down behind the counter. She unzipped her suitcase. The customs man flung out the brassieres and underpants that had been stuffed into the corners. His hands dove down along the sides and pulled out two wooden slats. He placed them on the shelf below his counter top. His hands plunged down again, spilling aside sweaters and scarves, and brought up two more slats.

"That's all," he said. "You may close it now."

Vannie bent down, gathered up her clothes and slapped them back into the suitcase. When she had finished, the customs man tied a baggage stub to the handle. Vannie watched the rolling luggage ramp carry the suitcase out of sight. Hardy helped her over the scale. "I'm all right," she assured him. "But maybe I ought to get some better-looking underwear."

"Did you have anything else in there, Vannie?"

"No, why?"

"They'll probably check it again before they put it on the plane."

Vannie handed over her currency declaration at the last counter. The three plainclothesmen were no longer there. Hardy flashed his diplomatic passport to an Aeroflot hostess standing guard at the bottom of the staircase.

"Oh, my God. My passport!" She ran back along the counters. The customs counter was unattended. On it, lying neatly, were her passport, ticket, boarding card, and baggage check. She clutched the documents and re-joined Hardy up in the departure lounge.

She waved the papers at him. "Nothing ever gets lost in this country by accident," she said, putting her document back in her bag.

"What did that customs man want with the sticks, Vannie?" Hardy asked.

"How should I know? Maybe he wants to build a house." Hardy didn't laugh.

"Don't be so serious," she said. "Maybe he thinks there are Kremlin secrets locked up in the hollows."

Then she saw the bearded figure in the belted raincoat striding from the VIP lounge toward the main departure gate, carrying his black attaché case of imported leather. Had he seen her coming up the stairs? She started to call him, then changed her mind. She had nothing more to say to Michael Petrov.

"Friend of yours?" Hardy asked.

"He's a friend of nobody's," Vannie answered.

"Was it his idea—the wooden sticks?"

"No. Mine."

Nancy was standing in front of the espresso machine at the buffet counter, waiting for service. Hardy was about to join her when Vannie tugged his arm, pulling him toward the glass wall looking out on the airfield. A Tupolev-124 was being fueled by a low oil truck, as a delegation of ten Chinese was boarding. Twenty yards behind, Petrov, alone, followed them up.

"Hardy," Vannie began. "I'll tell you. But only between you and me." She looped her arm in his, and in a low, tremulous voice, confided: "There's nothing, absolutely nothing in those wooden sticks. I set it up for them. A decoy. And they won't be sure there's nothing in them until after I've left Moscow. Hardy, oh, Hardy, I've won! I've beat them at their own stupid spying game."

"Christ, Vannie, haven't you played around enough?" He disentangled his arm from hers and signaled Nancy to forget the coffee. "Let's get you on the plane. Quick."

"But, Hardy, it wasn't just a game," Vannie protested, trying to catch up to his long strides.

"Vannie." He stopped abruptly and faced her. "Your friend Yuri Zhalkov was arrested last night at Lydia Chernova's studio."

The color drained from her cheeks. "Why?"

He shrugged his shoulders. "Witness to his uncle's murder. And he's not the only one. Up in Leningrad, they've arrested seven Army officers. So you see, Vannie, this is not quite the moment for children's theatrics."

"Hardy, I can't explain now . . . but I have . . . maybe I can. . . ." He had his hand under her elbow rushing her to the departure gate.

"Here's where we say good-bye, Vannie. You're boarding." He shook her hand.

Nancy gave her a hug. "Keep out of trouble till you get to Rome, please," she chided.

The three plainclothesmen were already on the field, standing in front of the Caravelle's wings. They watched her as she passed but made no move to stop her.

Vannie climbed the ladder to the Caravelle, grasping the strap of her shoulder bag. At the top of the ladder, she dipped her hand in and pulled out a white silk scarf.

The stewardess beckoned, *"Buona sera."*

Vannie turned and waved good-bye. With a last glance at the plainclothesmen, she ducked under the doorway.

They hadn't searched her handbag. She had waved, but they hadn't seen it. Walking down the blue-carpeted aisle, Vannie clutched her scarf, feeling beneath its silk sheath the black hardness of the Zhalkov cassette.

Chapter Seventeen

The bright summer houses along the Mediterranean were still shuttered. The high gusts of wind blowing in from the sea whipped the bushy tops of the lean pine trees. The foliage opened capriciously, admitting a shaggy warm patch of blue through the green umbrella. Ken turned off the country road toward the beach, parking the Fiat behind a deserted shack. He helped Vannie take off her boots, and they walked down toward the surf, crisp grains of sand rising up between their pale toes. Vannie arched her feet along the shoreline, letting them sink under the bubbly foam, timid pasty feet suddenly freed from airless months in padded boots.

It had been a three-hour flight to Rome—a clock hour's difference from Moscow but a light-year's difference in sound and color. Squinting at silver planes steaming in the orange sunshine, the violets sprinkled on lush green beds, Vannie had finally shut her eyes: Spring in Moscow was muddy brown. She had crouched in a corner of a taxi, trembling at the cacophony of city noises, voices and motors, bellowing horns on narrow streets. Moscow was silent.

She refused to talk in the hotel. "This isn't the Rossiya," Ken assured her. "It's the Rome Hilton." She shook her head. Exasperated, he drove her out to the beach at Fregene. Unwilling to be seduced by the Roman spring, Vannie hadn't changed her clothes, defiantly wearing her thick black Moscow suit as a proud emblem of winter hardship.

They walked into the wind, letting the sharp grains of sand prick their faces. "You did a terrible thing," Vannie began. "How could you leave Moscow with the Zhalkov story and not say a word to me? You didn't even know how that sheet of paper got into my bag. And then you go to London and leak the story to the London *Banner....*"

"Now, just a minute, Vannie. First of all, you'd never even heard of Zhalkov when I left Moscow. That paper in your shopping bag was written in Russian—which you can hardly read. It was meant for me."

"It certainly was. A real exclusive. A reporter's dream. What dropped out of my shopping bag, Kenneth L. Tomkins, was a KGB alibi, planted there by Simone Durand!"

"God save us from amateurs! Dear wife, I was perfectly aware of that even before I left Moscow."

Her voice was shrill, rising above the breakers. "You knew it was a plant? And you still made it public?"

"I didn't know it was Simone Durand, though that doesn't surprise me. But I didn't leak the story to anyone. When the KGB wants a story planted in the West, they have dozens of ways of getting it there. Your shopping bag was just one of many possible routes."

"Oh, Ken, then it wasn't you! I should have known better." With a low moan, she sank down into the sand. Ken sat down beside her, and she huddled against him, a black speck on an empty beach.

Without lifting her head, her voice a hoarse whisper, "How did you know the story was a fake?"

"Because I already knew the KGB murdered Zhalkov. Lydia told me. At Sasha Rabichov's. That's why she came."

"But who planted the story in London?"

"Mike Petrov. He sold it to the *Banner* a week before Rabichov's party with the promise that it wouldn't be printed until he was back in Moscow."

"That's impossible, Ken. It was Petrov himself who told me the story was a fake. It was Petrov who told me how Zhalkov was really assassinated. Ken, it was Petrov who gave me. . . . Ken, the evening Zhalkov was murdered, there was a tape running in his apartment that the KGB must have forgotten about. Do you understand what I'm saying? There is a recording of the murder, and I have a copy of it. Petrov gave it to me. It's here in my bag. Ken, he couldn't have done that and planted the fake KGB story at the same time!"

"Poor Vannie, I should never have taken you out of Binghamton."

"Don't treat me like a child! I have the cassette right here in my bag. Look at it. Touch it. It's all here!" Her voice cracked with suppressed rage.

Ken took the cassette and held it for a minute. "A tape recording of Zhalkov's murder?" Vannie nodded. Then

Ken handed it back to her. "No one will believe it, Vannie. Petrov plays both sides of the fence and takes his cut off each end. The *Banner* paid him five thousand dollars for the story. By the time he gave you that tape the truth about Zhalkov's death was a lost cause, and he knew it. He probably gave it to you as a way of squaring himself with the Army people."

"Petrov may think it's a lost cause, but I don't. And even if it is, I don't care. They've arrested Yuri Zhalkov, you know. Hardy Summers told me at the airport. And also seven officers in Leningrad who couldn't stomach the invasion of Czechoslovakia. The KGB is trying to blame the general's death on them. But this tape can prove they're innocent. We can help them!"

"Good God, Vannie, how the hell did you ever get involved in all this?"

"Oh, it's such a long story. I wouldn't even know how to begin." She looked up at his indulgent brown eyes. How much could she tell him? Everything? The address book, too? If he understood, would he forgive? If she were forgiven, would it make any difference? "If only people had told me things—before it all started. Told me about Petrov. About General Zhalkov."

"People do tell you things, Vannie. But you never listen . . . until it's too late."

"You never warned me about Simone Durand!"

"I did, Vannie. But you still found her fascinating."

"And Sasha Rabichov? Did you know the whole cocktail party was arranged by the KGB?"

"That's why I didn't want to go there in the first place."

"Then why did you let me persuade you? Why didn't you insist? I've been going to Sasha's for over a year. You never made any objection."

"You're a big girl, Vannie. Should I have locked you up in the apartment all day?"

"But Lydia and Yuri—I was just going there to pose. Did you know that Yuri was Zhalkov's nephew?"

"When Lydia told me the story at Sasha's, she told me who he was. You, Vannie, never even told me that you knew him."

"I didn't know his last name was Zhalkov."

"Why didn't you ask?"

"Because nobody in Moscow asks. It's always little Boris, or Sergei the poet, or Volodya with the beard. That's the way it is. You know that."

Ken nodded. "Sally Fields knew he was the general's nephew. She was supposed to have tea with him and en route two KGB types kidnapped her."

"Where did you learn that?"

"I ran into her in London yesterday, before I left for Rome. She was looking for publicity."

"Bitch. It was to our place that she was coming to have tea. I saw her the next day, and she never said a word. I asked Hardy Summers why she had to leave suddenly, and he put me off, too. You can't imagine what it was like those last ten days, Ken. Almost nobody gave me a straight answer to anything."

231

Ken picked up a handful of sand and let it spill down slowly through his fingers. "Tell me, under what statute did they arrest Yuri Zhalkov?"

"Hardy said he was accused of being a witness to the murder. Does that mean Siberia?"

"Maybe. If they really want to break him, they'll put him in an insane asylum."

"But they can't do that. He's not crazy."

"No," said Ken quietly. "They are."

"You know, these last ten days I thought I was going mad, too. This morning I thought I was holding onto my sanity by my fingertips. Ken, I asked myself, right after the takeoff, what would happen if I couldn't leave. If I had to live in that country the rest of my life. Like a Russian."

"Not the same, Vannie. The Russians are different. They've learned how to endure. You never had to."

"You mean I couldn't take it. I would end up in a nut house."

He brushed a windblown strand back from her forehead. "Luckily you haven't been put to the test."

"I have, and I've failed miserably. Now I'm here, away, free—but I don't feel free. I just feel I've copped out. Left my friends in the lurch. Ken, I'm still there really. I'm still all bound up in Moscow. Will that ever end?"

"Do you want it to?" he asked kindly.

Vannie didn't answer. They sat there quietly, brooding. The spring waves splashed harshly down below them, lapping up the dry sand, licking at their feet. They inched back, turning away from the darkening sea to watch the sunset.

Vannie got up first. "Come, I want you to hear the cassette. There must be something we can do."

Chapter Eighteen

Four windowless walls were unadorned save for a Kodacolor portrait of Richard Nixon. The rectangular fluorescent fixture, slatted by white plastic eggbox dividers, buzzed over the gray steel desk. On the desk lay a black and chrome tape recorder. Tilting the green leather chair backward against the wall, the square-jawed young man, his nose peeling from a recent suntan, listened rapturously to the Zhalkov cassette. At the final scratching sounds, he switched it off. He locked the tape recorder in the deep drawer at the side of his desk and dropped the key in his jacket pocket.

"Very interesting, Mrs. Tomkins. Yes, indeed." He was smiling to himself, his eyes still alert as if he were listening to his mind's playback. "Fascinating. Yes, indeed."

"I'm so glad you appreciate it, Mr. Smythe. It was a lot of trouble getting it out. But it was worth it, wasn't it?"

"Oh, yes. This fits into the picture beautifully," Mr. Smythe said.

"You mean you, too, realized the London *Banner* story was a fake?"

"A fake? Well, not entirely."

"But now that you have the cassette—the proof that the KGB killed Zhalkov—you know for sure that the story was a plant." She paused. "Don't you?"

"Why are you so certain, Mrs. Tomkins?"

"I've already explained it. I know the people involved."

"Yes, you did, didn't you? You were very . . . personally involved, weren't you, Mrs. Tomkins?"

"I suppose. I never learned how to be impersonally involved."

"One should always try, however difficult the circumstances. After all, you were an American living in an unfriendly foreign country. One must behave accordingly."

"I find my behavior irrelevant, Mr. Smythe. The important thing is that I brought the cassette out . . . I hope in time to save innocent people."

He smiled. "Don't you find it unusual that any Russian in this day and age should remain innocent?"

She smiled back. "I find it extraordinary, Mr. Smythe. And their courage even more so. That's why I think it's terribly important to make the story public."

"How do you intend to do that, Mrs. Tomkins?"

"Not me but my husband. His network would report the story with quote official government confirmation unquote. Then the Voice of America would broadcast it back into the Soviet Union. By the same route almost, you could undo the dirty work."

"But we haven't decided yet if the cassette is authentic," he interrupted.

"How long will that take?"

"Oh, it's a very long and complicated process. We have special information evaluators who do that work."

Vannie lit a cigarette. He took an ashtray out of the top drawer and slid it over to her. She took a deep puff. "A week?" He looked blank. "A month?"

"Don't ask me, Mrs. Tomkins. I have no idea."

"Well, all right. Whenever they decide that it's the truth, and it is the truth—that I'm certain of—then. . . ."

"Truth is a fascinating subject. Isn't it?" He flashed a broad grin; his large teeth were white and well tended. "But an attractive young woman like yourself shouldn't be discussing philosophy at ten o'clock in the morning." He pushed his chair back and came around to the front of the desk, towering over her. "May I buy you a cup of coffee downstairs? The cafeteria is open now."

"That's very kind, but I don't want coffee. Look, I don't want to be so persistent. But while your evaluators are . . . evaluating, or whatever evaluators do . . . innocent Russians are being arrested."

"You have many friends among them, don't you, Mrs. Tomkins?"

"Let's stop talking about my friends. I brought you the cassette because I thought you would want to help. I thought it was the American government's policy to encourage—officially or unofficially—the democratic spirit everywhere."

"Our agency has no such policy, Mrs. Tomkins. Our job is to further United States interests under any and all circumstances."

"And isn't it in the American interest to protect a few Russians who give a damn about freedom—especially when they're being framed?"

"Mrs. Tomkins, I regret to inform you, we are not the Boy Scouts."

Vannie stared at his large, cold eyes with disbelief. She crushed out her cigarette and got up. "Good-bye, Mr. Smythe. My husband will report the Zhalkov cassette without official backing." She extended her hand. He held it.

"If I were your husband, I wouldn't do that, Mrs. Tomkins."

She disengaged her hand. "You can't prevent him."

"There are many things we can prevent if we choose to."

"Like the arrest of innocent Army officers," she flared.

He smiled. "Maybe. If it's in our interest. At the moment, we prefer that the story in the London *Banner* stand. Unrefuted."

"But it's a fake."

"That, Mrs. Tomkins, is quite irrelevant."

She clutched at her bag, her fingers grasping the leather straps. "My God, I've gone from one madhouse to another. Or maybe I'm crazy."

"Now, now, Mrs. Tomkins," he said soothingly. "You see, you are still overwrought. It was a very trying experience for you in Moscow. In Leningrad, too. You still have to rest. To recover completely." He led her to the door.

"Oh, by the way . . . I have something for you." He slipped his hand inside his breast pocket and pulled out a manila business envelope. He ripped it open at the side.

"I believe this is yours," he said softly as he handed Vannie her red leather address book.